FLiRTiN'
with the
MONSTER

Other Titles in the Smart Pop Series

Your Favorite Authors on Ellen Hopkins'
Crank and *Glass*

Edited and Original Introduction by Ellen Hopkins

with Leah Wilson

An imprint of BenBella Books, Inc.

Dallas, TX

Smart Pop is an imprint of BenBella Books, Inc.
10440 N. Central Expy., Suite 800
Dallas, TX 75231
www.benbellabooks.com
Send feedback to feedback@benbellabooks.com

Smart Pop and BenBella are federally registered trademarks.

Printed in the United States of America

Library of Congress Cataloging-in-Publication Data is available for this title.
ISBN 978-1933771-67-0

Proofreading by Jennifer Canzoneri
Cover design by Sammy Yuen Jr.
Text design and composition by PerfecType, Nashville, TN

Special discounts for bulk sales are available. Please contact
bulkorders@benbellabooks.com.

Table of Contents

Introduction

Ellen Hopkins

The years between 1995 and 2002 were a time of great personal chaos. My marriage was rocky. My finances were shaky. I had a young child to raise, at a time when I thought I would be free of parental responsibility. I had been lied to. Stolen from. Left deeply in debt. And figuratively slapped in the face by the very person largely at fault for the turmoil in my life—my middle child and oldest daughter, "Kristina"[1]—and her decision to flirt with the monster drug methamphetamine, or crystal meth.

---

[1] "Kristina" is not her real name. But to afford her some measure of privacy, she will be referred to as Kristina throughout this book, including in the byline of the essay she contributed. Where appropriate, other important players will be referred to by their real names. If names are in quotation marks, they are pseudonyms, used for the sake of anonymity.

Flirtin' with the Monster

It wasn't a new story. Many parents lose their children to addiction. On the flip side, many children lose their parents to substance abuse. The problem is multigenerational, and will continue to be until we can educate our youth honestly about drugs, and how they affect not only the user, but also everyone who loves him or her, not to mention society in general. My generation to a large degree led the charge toward "it's my life, I'll do what I want with it" experimentation, and my own teen years weren't completely untouched by the "sex, drugs, and rock 'n' roll" credo.

But this was my child. My beautiful, brilliant, talented daughter. The A+ student with an amazing artistic gift and the potential to not only dream big, but to realize her dreams. Instead, with one wrong turn, her dreams disintegrated, one by one. And, despite every effort to turn her around, she would never be the same.

When her slide started, it didn't take long to recognize that something was up. She had never brought home anything less than an A, and within a few weeks of her summer fling[2] we saw her grades begin to drop steadily. Okay, a couple of Bs weren't so bad. It was high school, after all. But Cs? Something was up. And Ds? She was in major trouble.

Before that realization, however, there were other signs. Her attitude shift, for one. Arguing with her little sister more and more often. (The two had always been tight, but now it seemed they had little in common.) Holing herself up in her room. Purposely letting her chores go. Being mean to the dogs. Yelling. Screaming. Cursing,

---

[2] As depicted in *Crank*.

even. After awhile, pretty much telling my husband, John, and me where we could go.

But the first solid clue was the persistent aroma of cigarettes. No one in the house smoked, so when that awful lingering scent of stale tobacco kept clinging to Kristina, we knew she had been smoking, despite her denials that it was "someone else," "someone in the car," "someone standing next to me," etc. Of course, she got careless and we found cigarettes in her pockets. And that made us look harder.

I'm not sure what I expected to find. Pot, probably. Most of my own adolescent counterculture partying involved marijuana. It was readily available when I was in high school, as were psychedelics like mushrooms and peyote. I'll admit to sampling those as well, though I didn't find the "high" particularly enjoyable. I didn't like the feeling of not being in control of my mind. And I never really saw drugs like cocaine or speed, except for the occasional "diet pill."[3]

Meth, I know now, was around then. But it never crossed my path. So when we started investigating Kristina's increasingly unstable behavior, I truly believed we'd find something much less devastating. Something controllable. Something easily left behind. What we discovered plunged us into a living nightmare, one that lasted seven years, until Kristina finally went to prison.

Kristina says in her own essay here that the whole runaway ride started as she sought acceptance. What she didn't realize was that

---

[3] Fortunately, I don't seem to carry the addictive gene or predisposition to addiction. When I chose to get married and have children (at age nineteen), it was easy enough to leave the party scene behind. Today, while I do enjoy a good glass of red wine, I don't use drugs, including prescription drugs.

the only acceptance that truly mattered was that of her family. Her so-called friends all had personal agendas—sex, drugs, connections to dealers. One of her juvenile detention counselors told her flat out, "Kristina, the stoners accept everyone. How does that make you special?" At that point, she was already too far gone to care, and her family—the people who truly loved and accepted her, just as she was—had begun to close themselves off from her, out of sheer self-defense.

Many addicts believe that their addiction belongs to them and them alone. But truly, their addiction belongs to everyone who loves them. Their parents. Siblings. Children. Partners. Friends. In my author's note at the beginning of *Crank*, I say, "It is hard to watch someone you love fall under the spell of a substance that turns him or her into a stranger. Someone you don't want to know." I would add that the pain of watching that person choose slow, certain death never really goes away. When Kristina was finally sent to prison, it made me happy because she was dying, killing herself, and nothing but lockup was going to stop her imminent demise.

She was safe,[4] and so was society, at least from her. She went to prison not on drug charges but for identity theft, fraud, and check kiting—things she did to support her habit. Later, she told me that she and "Trey" used to walk wealthy neighborhoods, scoping out mailboxes for credit card or bank statements, checks, etc., that they could "borrow." Sometimes they broke into houses and stole these

---

[4] As safe as you can be in state prison, living with murderers and drug traffickers, some of whom she might have crossed paths with before, and perhaps even owed money to.

things. That included my house.[5] I had no clue about that until a local supermarket called to tell me "some young woman" was trying to cash one of my checks and the ID[6] looked suspicious. We discovered checks missing from the bottom of the box (clever!). But there was more. All my jewelry was gone (including the heirlooms my mother left me when she died), plus cameras, video equipment, etc. These things were pawned, and never recovered.

Despite a certain amount of relief at her being taken off the street, I also felt a lot of anger, confusion, and guilt. Why did she choose that particular path? What part did I play in her choices? Could I somehow have stopped her? Turned her around?

People often ask why I chose to write *Crank*. Why open our windows, let strangers peek inside and learn our secrets? My answer is: I didn't start the book with strangers in mind. I started it for me, to gain some understanding and answers to my questions. I chose to write from Kristina's POV because my point of view didn't matter. I needed to climb inside *her* head and look at *her* world through *her* eyes. As I wrote, I did gain some personal enlightenment, and accepted that the decisions she made were her own.

---

[5] Also her house, until she moved out at eighteen. She moved back in for awhile, when Orion was a baby. There is a scene in *Glass* where Kristina is crashed out on the floor and the baby is in danger, so her mom kicks her out. A variation of that scene really happened.

[6] One time I asked her how she managed to rent an apartment, considering the state of her finances. She told me she just got a fake ID. I had no idea that one had MY name on it. When she was arrested, she had several, with a variety of names.

A bigger outcome of the writing process was that I began to see how important this story was, and that it might mean something to more people than just me. To open it to a larger audience, I chose to fictionalize, which allowed me enough distance from real situations and players to draw the wide-angle picture without worrying about how accurate the details were. "Truth," after all, is colored by perception. Few enough memoirs are 100 percent true. And changing names, locations, or genders, sometimes even creating composite characters, afforded at least a small sense of anonymity to real people whose lives might be affected.[7]

When I started the book, I was already eking out a living as a freelance writer and non-fiction children's book author. I had dabbled with picture books and chapter books, and had written a decent novel, none of which I ever interested a publisher in. I had also written poetry pretty much my entire life. I knew I was a good writer and a decent poet. But I had no idea I belonged writing YA verse novels, much less that I could realize bestselling success.

I met Julia Richardson, then an editor with Simon & Schuster,[8] at a book festival. I showed her a few pages, which is all I had written at the time. It was a fortunate turn of events, because she had recently read an article about the growing meth problem. That, coupled with her opinion that my writing was really good, sent a contract my way. The book was published in October 2004. It took a while for readers to find the book, then pass it on, again and again.

---

[7] Some of these people (family members, for the most part) have been "outed" over time.

[8] Now at Houghton Mifflin.

The climb to *New York Times* bestseller took two and half years, quite unusual in publishing, but a testament to the power of the story. And now nothing for *me* will ever be the same.

Today, all five of my novels have achieved the coveted designation "*New York Times* bestseller." Two, *Crank* and *Glass*, are loosely based on our story. The others are as powerful because I choose to write about issues—suicide, physical and sexual abuse, cutting, depression, rape, prostitution—that many other authors shun. My critics call me on that, saying the subject matter is too mature for my audience, or even gratuitous. To that I say *pthpthpthpthpthpthpth. . .* or however you write a resounding raspberry. These issues touch lives every day, including the lives of children and teens. It's important to write about them honestly because only then can we gain insight into not only the victims, but also the perpetrators. Without that understanding, we can't hope to change things for the better.

Would I have chosen this particular path to success? Surely not. Every day still brings worry for Kristina, who has some brain damage, and a benign tumor in the part of the brain that the drug affected. She struggles to make ends meet, flitting from one minimum wage job to another. Between two years in prison and four in programs, she managed to stay clean for six years, only to relapse. Another pregnancy[9] made her clean up again, but she will always be an addict and have to fight the desire to return to the drug. She

---

[9] Her fifth. Only the youngest two, who she had after her release from prison, live with her. John and I adopted Orion, age twelve. Jade (the baby she was pregnant with at the end of *Glass*), now ten, lives with her aunt. Heaven, age seven, lives with her other grandparents.

is the anchor that keeps me grounded whenever I start to feel the slightest bit lofty about what I have achieved.

There is another price for my success, one I pay gratefully. Every day brings scores of e-mails and other messages.[10] Many simply tell me how wonderful my books are.[11] Others thank me for teaching them to enjoy reading, perhaps for the first time ever. A good number thank me for giving them that all-important understanding of the issues I write about.[12] And then there are the ones that ask for help, either for themselves or for someone they care about. These often start out with, "I don't know why I'm coming to you, other than you seem like someone who will listen when no one else will. . . ."

I do listen. I always ask if there's someone close to them who they can go to for help—a teacher, counselor, relative, or friend who can intervene if necessary. Once in awhile, I feel I must personally step in and initiate the intervention.[13] It can be a heavy burden, but it is one I shoulder without complaint because I feel it is simply part of the deal.

See, one morning right in the midst of those seven years of chaos, I was walking down our long, steep driveway to get the newspaper. It was just past dawn, and the sky was salmon pink. I looked

---

[10] Through MySpace, Facebook, etc.

[11] I like these, of course, especially the ones that say I'm their favorite author, ever. Yay.

[12] Usually because they have been personally affected by these things, in whatever ways.

[13] I prefer not to. But a handful of times, it was the only way to get these people the help they needed.

toward the Sierra, appreciating the beauty, and feeling the presence of the Creator. So I threw an offer in his/her direction. "If you help me make sense of this, help me dig out of this place and maybe realize a little success, I swear I'll work my butt off for you."

I've been working my butt off ever since. Lesson learned: Never pray lightly. Someone just might be listening.

PART I

Do not come lightly
to this hallowed place.
Dare not brandish

                    words

as swords, lest they turn
on you. Seek not fame
nor fortune, ethereal
by nature, for both

                    are

winged. Write, bent
beneath the weight
of honesty. For it is
there your words gain

                    power.

Like most writers, my early attempts at storytelling were formulaic—I attempted to write like authors whose work I admired, and pretty much failed because trying to emulate voice is an exercise in futility. But I did keep at it, and eventually I found my own unique way of putting words on paper and discovered the importance of writing straight from the heart. There, in the pulsing depths of my ventricles, my words found power.

I am thrilled to bring the power of words to an ever-growing audience. My core readership is American teens, ages fourteen to eighteen. But that nucleus is expanding. I have heard from readers as young as eleven, and as old as seventy-five. Kids have shared my books with their parents, and grandparents. Soldiers have carried them to Iraq, and sailors have taken them 300 feet below the Atlantic, on nuclear submarines. They have found their way to other countries, near and far. I am amazed to hear from readers in Australia, Germany, Japan, Nicaragua, and the Philippines. How incredible to know my words have touched so many lives.

On a professional level, there is a certain satisfaction in gaining critical acclaim. A good review feeds the ego. A starred review makes you practically giddy. Awards, of course, are major strokes. So far, I haven't been invited up any red carpets, wearing Dior and dripping diamonds. But my books have been given top honors by readers, librarians, teachers, and booksellers. Each means I have risen above formula, to a special place of my own.

Beyond all that, there is a real sense of accomplishment when someone you respect because of their own contributions to literature or society-at-large reads your books and takes something positive away from that experience. Here, a group of my peers talks about their takeaway from reading my books. Plus, a substance abuse counselor and a criminal court judge discuss the insights *Crank* and *Glass* have given them, and others. How gratifying is that?

Shall I create
for you a perfect world
where you can safely wander?
Society scrubbed sterile,
free from imperfections?

Should I dream
for you characters who
never make mistakes?
Conflict lacking conflict?
A faultless human race?

Do I strive
to please the gatekeepers
who'd rather close their eyes?
Or does a candid glimpse
of underbelly truly serve you better?

My books are often challenged, and sometimes banned, by "gate-keepers" (librarians, teachers, or parents) who believe they serve the best interest of young adult readers by choosing what they may or may not read. While their hearts might be in the right place, does this sort of censorship really serve its intended purpose? And should YA authors write sanitized subject matter, with the gatekeepers in mind? Niki Burnham offers her opinion.

Role Models

Niki Burnham

I write books about teenagers, primarily for teenagers (though teen-savvy adults read them, too). Some of the books have stylized cartoon covers, tipping off the reader that what's on the pages is comedy. Despite that, over the years I've received many letters from concerned parents, questioning whether or not my books are appropriately shelved. They cite the fact that some of the characters use foul language, that one character has a gay mother, or that one character smokes (ignoring the fact that she quits) in support of their argument that my writing is a "bad influence" on teen readers.

I'm often taken to task for not living up to my "responsibility" as an author to provide teenagers with good role models.

While I understand their concerns, I believe that attempting to limit teens' reading to "good role models" is the wrong way to go about educating teens about the world in which we all live.

When sitting down to craft a story, an author's primary responsibility is to the reader—not to any gatekeeper, be that person a librarian, bookseller, publisher, *New York Times* book reviewer, or even a parent. The author's job is to give a book's intended readers an engrossing story about believable—and therefore imperfect—characters. When that happens, I believe that any other responsibility an author may have to protect teens from the dangers of the world falls into place. However, I do not believe the reverse is always true. A book about perfect characters—who never skip school, wouldn't think of trying a cigarette, and don't hang out with a so-called "bad" crowd—may please parents or others who believe teens should only be exposed to positive role models, but it won't necessarily please actual readers. They won't identify personally with the main character, which means they won't go along for the ride, seeing the world through that character's eyes. A perfect character doesn't experience true conflict. There are no real challenges that must be overcome: no social dilemmas, no moral crises, no testing of their mettle. The perfect character will always make the right choice in any situation. Therefore, the story isn't believable.

This is true no matter the author and no matter the age of the intended audience for a book. For example, when the intended reader is three years old, a story about a bunny whose mother loves him even when he misbehaves and runs away is believable. Toddlers relate to Margaret Wise Brown's *The Runaway Bunny* and his desire to be free—which isn't role model behavior when you're three—because they can see themselves in the actions of a bunny who tells his mother he's leaving, he cannot be found, and that he's never coming home. (My own four-year-old niece often tells her father, "I'm not talking to you again! Ever. In. My. Life!" Her next words usually come within a five-minute time frame, accompanied by a sheepish smile.)

Toddlers learn—right along with the bunny, whose desire to be free of controlling parents mirrors toddlers' own occasional desires—that running away isn't the wisest thing to do. They're also reassured by the loving reaction of the bunny's mother at the end of the story. The bunny makes a mistake, and his mother loves him anyway.

The story is engrossing, because the reader wants to know what happens next. It's believable, because the emotions are true to life. Toddlers love *The Runaway Bunny*, and over the years, adults of all stripes have loved it too. And in addressing the entertainment needs of the intended reader by creating an imperfect main character, the author also addresses the concerns of gatekeepers who want readers to come away with a lesson. If the story featured a bunny who nodded and did as he was told when his mother simply said, "Running away is bad. It can be dangerous," it might please gatekeepers who want children to come away with that message. But would it satisfy kids? I don't believe it would.

By the teen years, life has become more complex, and the stories teens read should reflect that reality. Teens are well aware that, in the real world, people aren't perfect. People swear. They hurt others' feelings. They lie. They struggle with knowing the right thing to do in situations that don't have simple black-and-white answers. They learn that actions have consequences.

Teens don't learn about life from characters who are perfect; they learn from those who are imperfect. When a book is so sanitized that it contains only perfect characters, or characters whose role in the story is merely to teach the reader a lesson, that book no longer rings true to the intended audience. It gets tossed aside, unread, and rightfully so. It's no different than a book where the bunny learns his lesson when his mother tells him, "No. Don't do that."

I'm not saying that an author—any author—should be graphic or shocking just for the sake of being graphic or shocking. That's not good storytelling, because it's not (here's that word again!) *believable*. Teens are smart. They know when a product is being overhyped and turn away. They crave characters whose innermost emotions and external reactions ring true, whether those fictional characters show up on the pages of a comedy, a dark drama, or a story about an alternate universe. The stronger the ring of truth in a story, the more teens gravitate toward reading it.

And that's a good thing, because it educates teens about the world in which they live.

Ellen Hopkins' books are known for their gritty realism. In *Crank*, there's a scene where the main character, Kristina, sits in a hospital waiting room. She's just visited an acquaintance who's near death after a drug-induced fall, and is scared out of her wits. Yet while she's sitting in the waiting room, she's thinking,

I needed
to go home
'cause somewhere
deep down

I needed
my mommy.

And all that made me really
really need

a line.

My guess is that, if some parents are concerned about having their teens exposed to a fictional, temporary cigarette smoker in what's obviously a romantic comedy, those same parents would just about go over the edge upon discovering that their teen was reading about a meth user who flirts recklessly with strange guys, drives while high, skips school, and sneaks out of the house at night. A meth user who can look at someone her own age lying in a hospital bed, mangled as a direct result of drug use, and think to herself, "I really really need a line." An imperfect character who's as far from a positive role model as you can get.

Parents have every right to be concerned about what their kids are reading. They pay attention to their teens' friends, activities, and day-to-day behavior because they care. They look at what's on the news each night and think, "I need to protect my child from this."

So when they see a thick, black book on their teenager's nightstand with the word "Crank" emblazoned on the front in white powder, it's natural for alarm bells to go off. They wonder—understandably—why their teen would ever want to read about a meth addict, especially for five hundred-plus pages. Is there something going on with their teen? Something they should know?

Should they give their teen something else to read? Something that helps them attain their goal of protecting their child?

I'd argue that those caring parents do their teens a greater service by allowing them to read whatever they want and making it clear they're willing and available to discuss it with them afterward: protecting them by preparing them.

I doubt any study could show that toddlers who read *The Runaway Bunny* have a higher runaway rate than the general toddler population. Similarly, reading about meth use—or sex, cheating, shoplifting, or any other number of reckless behaviors—isn't the same as engaging in that behavior. In fact, it better prepares teens for when they're faced with a decision that could change their lives.

Rational teens will read that scene in *Crank*, imagine the antiseptic smell of the waiting room, visualize a rail-thin teen with tubes protruding from her nose and arms, hear the doctors whispering about what may be left of that teen's brain, and think, *Who in the world would risk that?*

On the other hand, Kristina's reaction is, "I need a line."

The complete irrationality of Kristina's behavior spurs readers to think, *Is she crazy?*

What Hopkins does, in just those few paragraphs, is show readers how irrational and overwhelming addiction to meth can be. Why crank is known as "the monster." How it affects judgment and leads users to do things they'd never, ever do when off the drug. And right there, readers make the decision never to try meth, because they've seen what it did to Kristina, someone who, in many ways, is like them or someone they know.

Teenagers hear all kinds of things about drugs, no matter where they live or what school they attend. No parent can keep their teen from hearing stories from their peers, from seeing a commercial for a *60 Minutes* story on the surge in meth use, from witnessing an emaciated drug user crash their car in the grocery store parking lot. Their curiosity is bound to be piqued. But even if parents have made it clear to their teen that they are willing to talk to him or her about anything—even drug use—teens want to be informed without being *compelled* to go to their parents and ask, "So, what do you know about meth, Mom?"

Most teens know that if they ask such a question, their parents will wonder, *Who's telling Janey about meth? Are kids at school using? Which of Janey's friends might be using?* If a friend *is* using, will their parents pressure them to stop seeing that friend? Even teens who have great relationships with their parents may hesitate before asking such a question.

In addition to simple curiosity, teens want to prove—both to themselves and to their parents—that they can comprehend adult issues on their own. They're at a point in their lives where they feel like adults, and where they're often given adult responsibilities. They manage their own schedules, work after-school jobs, manage their own money, and have ever-increasing amounts of time away from adult supervision. They're in a position to make their own decisions about many aspects of their lives. Therefore, their first instinct isn't always to run to their parents with questions about an issue they feel they can figure out themselves.

Maybe they'll watch a bit of that *60 Minutes* story. Maybe they'll go on the internet and find a website with reliable medical information about the effects of meth use. Maybe not.

But if they have access to a book like *Crank*, the learning experience is different, more immediate. Reading fiction allows them to learn vicariously through the eyes of a character who's been there. A character who's their age, attending a school bearing similarities to their own, with friends who may be like people they know. In other words, by seeing meth use from the viewpoint of a character who's *believable*, they see why the character makes poor choices and then see the consequences of those choices. In doing so, they educate themselves—without a lecture, and without reading pages of dry medical information—about a topic like meth use, something their parents may not completely understand themselves.

The other benefit of encouraging teens to learn by picking up a book? They can read it in the safety of their own bedroom, where they can take their time thinking about the character's experience. Where friends aren't exerting any peer pressure. Where parents are available should they have questions. Where they can put the book down if they feel they're not ready for it. And where they can pick it up again whenever they are.

It's a far better situation than learning about meth from a friend of a friend—one who may not have the facts straight—during a conversation in the school cafeteria. Or, worse, when they're faced with it unexpectedly at a party, at an after-school job, or—as in Kristina's case—while visiting out-of-town relatives who turn out to be drug users themselves. Or who live in a building with cute boys who use and who can be awfully persuasive.

In *Crank*, readers see that Kristina was woefully uninformed about meth before she tried it the first time. She didn't know what it'd do to her. She didn't know how hard it'd be to kick after she tried it just once. She was having a bad day, feeling lonely, and a boy paid attention to her. What could doing one little line hurt when the boy offering it was so sweet?

Informed teens are far less reckless than Kristina. Any teen who's read *Crank* or its sequel, *Glass*, is going to have an instant, powerful reaction to any invitation to try meth. They'll be far more likely to say no and walk away—even if they're feeling lonely and being told that one little line will make them feel better—because they've seen, through Kristina's eyes, what will happen to them if they do. They may or may not be raped while high, as Kristina was, but they'll know from her experience that their judgment will be seriously affected. They'll know that their personality will change, and that they may lose the very essence of who they are.

They'll know that everything they've worked to attain at that point in their lives—a good academic record, a spot on a sports team, a turn as a soloist in a recital, savings from an after-school job, and even their friendships—may all go up in (pardon the pun) smoke if they try it even one time.

They'll also have a healthy appreciation of meth's power to completely addict them on the very first try. They'll know because it happened to Kristina—someone very much like them or someone they might know—and they experienced the consequences through her.

If they're lucky, maybe it was even an adult who handed them the book in the first place, saying, "Read this. It has an engrossing plot and a believable, interesting main character. You'll love it." Just like they loved *The Runaway Bunny* when they were three.

Niki Burnham is the RITA Award–winning author of six novels for teens, including the Royally Jacked series, *Sticky Fingers*, and *Goddess Games*. She lives in Massachusetts. You can find her online at www. nikiburnham.com.

For whom does she write,
this poet, transformed?
Why craft fiction
with sparsely-worded metaphor?
Why bother with assonance,
alliteration, form, diction?

Not for awards. One librarian's Printz
is another's bird cage liner.
Nor does she write
for critics, who call her too tough.
Overreaching. Too poetic.
Not nearly poetic enough.

And how can she hope
to please an audience as passionate
and diverse as the suns and moons
and satellites strewn across
this vast universe? She might
tell you she writes for all of these,
or none. For this poet, like all poets,
writes true to herself.

With every book an author writes, he or she has choices to make. How to tell this particular story? Past or present tense? From whose point of view? How long should it be? What format serves it best? A first novel can be especially difficult to craft and find an audience for. Some might argue I made all the wrong choices with *Crank*—a first novel, loosely based on fact, told first person, in verse? Susan Hart Lindquist tells why she thinks it worked.

More Than Just a Broken Line

Susan Hart Lindquist

These days, when talking about why a book "works" one can't simply take into account the compelling story or the beauty of the writing. Today, part of what makes a book work is its ability to connect with an audience. To become a bestseller. To stay in print.

For some authors, this has turned the game of publishing into a psychological tug of war between the desire to remain true to one's creative vision and the need to consider what it takes to publish and, in turn, connect with readers. *Do I want to write "for me" or must I write "for them"? How can I choose? How can I do both? If I write "for them" will I be selling out?*

It's a conundrum to be sure, and I confess, at times I've been torn by these questions. Perhaps that's why I was skeptical when Ellen first told me about the young adult novel she was writing. "It's about my daughter's addiction," she said. "And I'm thinking of writing it in verse."

A first novel in verse starring her daughter on drugs? Sounded risky to me. Experience teaches us that personal stories rarely interest others, and that a story about your own teen's trouble with drugs could easily slip into becoming a preachy, cautionary tale that no one would want to read. Putting those drawbacks together in a not-always-popular verse format could make for a very hard sell.

But Ellen remained steadfast, went ahead with her plan, sold her book before it was even finished, and the rest is history, isn't it? When *Crank* was released in 2004, it "quickly drew readers, rising to top 10 lists within six weeks of publication."[1] Now, it and its sequel, *Glass*, are not just selling, they're *best* selling. Recently, Ellen was referred to as "one of the bestselling (if not the bestselling) living poets in the country."[2]

How did *that* happen? The books are not only written in verse, they're long. The heroine is far from heroic, the endings are not

---

[1] www.ellenhopkins.com
[2] From Galleycat's "Kids Are Reading Poetry, Even If Adults Don't Recognize the Poets" (http://www.mediabistro.com/galleycat/trends/kids_are_reading_poetry_even_if_adults_dont_recognize_the_poets_85602.asp)

happy, the format is unusual, and often the vocabulary can be challenging. Yet kids are buying them. And they're not only buying them, they're actually *reading* them, and not just the way I might have "read" a very long book in verse when I was a teen (scan the first few pages, flip through to find the graphic parts, carry it around with me to look cool). No, they're reading, quoting, memorizing, reciting, acting, rereading, and falling in love—not only with the books and their "heroine" Kristina, but often with Ellen herself.[3]

Your first thoughts might be, "Yes, that's easy to understand. Reviews have been favorable, even glowing. The covers scream 'commercial.' And then there's the edgy subject matter. The dark true story. Kristina herself. And Bree . . ."

Of course, absolutely. Story, character, a book's cover—who can deny these make a huge contribution to a book's success?[4] But look beneath the veil of striking covers, troubled teen, and dark story of addiction. Look closely and you'll discover something more is drawing readers to Ellen's books: the writing.

Okay, I confess—I've had this conversation before with other authors who've read *Crank* and *Glass*, and even with some who haven't. "What?" they scoff, pooh-poohing the idea that the popularity of any commercially successful young adult fiction could actually be rooted in the *writing*. Yes, the writing, but more specifically the *choices* behind

---

[3] Check the thousands of testimonials posted by "friends" on Ellen's MySpace page (www.myspace.com/ellenhopkins).
[4] The Harry Potter and Twilight series come to mind . . .

the writing.[5] Examine a few and you'll discover that in writing *for me* Ellen has actually written *for them* and made a connection with readers most writers only dream of—all without Oprah Winfrey, a publisher-driven marketing blitz, or even starred reviews.[6]

Consider her choice of story. When she could have written a more predictably marketable tale derived from her many other interests,[7] she chose instead to write one that had to have been difficult to tell, as painful and personal and unresolved as the story is. But she wrote it because, as she explains, "I had to tell the story for myself."[8]

For myself. Certainly, it could have been as it is for many writers, that this story begged to be written. Sometimes a story pushes in beside everything else you try to put down on paper. An idea won't leave you alone. It speaks to you, interrupts, shouts and teases, or whispers to you in dreams or while you're at the dentist. *What about me? What about me?*

Or perhaps Ellen just needed to get the story off her chest, to be done with it, to free herself from it. Each of these reasons may have played a part in her choice, but I imagine for her it was more

---

[5] As every author knows, writing is about choices. Which story? For whom? Which viewpoint? Present tense or past? First person viewpoint or third? In chapters? Sections? Verse? What about dialogue? Transitions? Character development? Voice? Simile? Metaphor? Words?

[6] Ellen's new book *Identical* has just garnered starred reviews from *Kirkus* and *Publishers Weekly*—her first.

[7] On her website she mentions interest in hiking, biking, fishing, camping, gardening, barrel racing, dance, and raising German Shepherds. Her nonfiction books include subjects such as orcas, aliens, and rain forests.

[8] From Kate Pavao's article "Ellen Hopkins" in the Sept 8, 2007, Children's Bookshelf from *Publishers Weekly*

as Isak Dinesen said, that "All sorrows can be borne if you put them into a story or tell a story about them."[9] Writing *Crank* was cathartic,[10] therapeutic; putting the story onto paper helped ease her pain and helped her make sense of what had happened to her family.

Notice, however, that in neither *Crank* nor *Glass* is there even a remote hint of a self-indulgent, poor-me tale about guilt or regret, or the author's own reflection. Though in some secret place Ellen may have once harbored the idea that what happened to her daughter could have been avoided if she'd done things differently, a treatise on the mistakes she made as a mother play no part in the story she had to tell. She did not decide to write a testimonial, an exposé, or self-help book for concerned parents. She didn't write a women's novel, or even a collection of poetry. As personal as this story is, she did not choose to write it as *her* story. She wrote it as Kristina's. And she wrote it with a young adult audience in mind.

But why, even though Ellen regularly published magazine articles and authored more than twenty non-fiction books for young readers before writing *Crank*, did she decide not to write the *true* story about her daughter? It's not as if she used fiction to invent a happy ending. The obvious reason is simple: she may be her mother and may have been present for a great deal of what happened in her daughter's life, but she *isn't* "Kristina." Writing "the truth" about her would have been tricky, even impossible, not to mention just a tad

---

[9] I've lifted all author quotes from www.thinkexist.com or *Writers on Writing*.
[10] From an interview with Ellen, "Interview: Sculpting the Words Behind *Glass*," by R.J. Carter

presumptuous. Another less obvious reason is that she knew better. As a seasoned writer, Ellen must have been aware that it's ill-advised to try to write a story exactly as it happened simply because it can make for very dull and tedious reading. In order to involve readers and entertain them, "a writer must be conscious of drama and heighten events and even change them."[11]

Yes, change for dramatic effect is a valid reason to fictionalize a true story.[12] But a better reason has more to do with what's true about the lie you end up telling. Authors as different from one another in their treatment of ideas as Stephen King and Edward Albee offer guidance. For King, "Fiction is the truth inside the lie." For Albee, "A good writer turns fact into truth." Walking the line between "accuracy" and "honesty" is what fiction writers *do*. Facts give a piece credibility, but *honesty* brings credibility to the author and, in turn, trust from readers. Ellen herself says she writes "with honesty, from a place of deep respect for my readers."[13]

A less obvious reason for her to have written her books as fiction has to do with her choice of viewpoint. While she could have written from a third-person point of view that would have allowed her more creative distance and objectivity, she chose to write in first-person fixed point of view, in which the "I" protagonist is the central narrator, the center of action, and the filter through which the fictional world is experienced.

---

[11] From Pat Kubis and Bob Howland's *Writing Fiction, Nonfiction, and How to Publish*

[12] As long as you acknowledge that it *is* fiction, re: James Frey's debacle.

[13] From "Interview with Ellen Hopkins," *Barnes & Noble*

First person "is the voice of authority, seeming to record an actual true life experience."[14] It's close up and intimate—for the writer *and* for the reader. By putting herself into Kristina's shoes, Ellen invites readers to do the same and opens the door for them to come closer, to climb inside the heart and mind of the main "I" character.

In her own words, Ellen says, "Writing from my daughter's point of view helped me understand the decisions she made and my part in them."[15] But not really being Kristina, how could she know what her daughter felt or what made her do what she did? Author Grace Paley gave this advice to writers: "Write *from* what you know *into* what you don't know." Author Carlos Fuentes has said that "Bad books are about things the writer already knew before he wrote them." Even painter Georgia O'Keefe understood that one makes art, "To make your unknown known."

Clearly, we write to discover as much as we write to reveal. But coming to that discovery is another matter. How do we get there? How do we find our way to this "known," this "truth"? For some writers, it's often about voice, which can be a kind of magical doorway into character and story. For readers, voice is one of the most important elements of writing because it creates a pathway between author and reader.

Yes, when we refer to an author's "voice," we're sometimes talking about the author's style, the "quality that makes his or her writing unique, and which conveys the author's attitude, personality, and character." But voice is also "the characteristic speech and thought

---

[14] From *Writing Fiction, Nonfiction, and How to Publish*
[15] From "Interview: Sculpting the Words Behind Glass"

patterns of a first person narrator; a persona"[16]—a voice particular to a story, one a writer often hears speaking in his head.[17]

It's not magic all the time, however, at least not at first. Choosing the right voice can be problematic. Sometimes the one you're listening to just isn't "right." That's what happened for Ellen, who felt the original voice in *Crank* was "too strong, too angry" until she decided to write in verse. "When I discovered verse novel as a viable format (hearing Sonya Sones speak at a conference), I knew immediately that's how *Crank* should be written."[18]

"Verse is very interior . . . Writing in verse puts me deeply inside my characters' heads and hearts."[19] Simply put, writing in first person and writing in verse allowed her to "become" Kristina.

And verse seems an organic fit for a poet becoming novelist.[20] Writing in stanzas probably felt comfortable, familiar. But easy? Hardly. "There are people who think it's easier to write books in verse, and it's definitely not. *Crank* took me about a year to write, and most of that was developing the style and formatting." Telling a

---

[16] From "Definition of Voice," by Ginny Wiehardt (http://fictionwriting.about.com/od/glossary/g/voice.htm)

[17] Writing, as it was for Faulkner, is often a matter of listening to the voices.

[18] From "Interview with Ellen Hopkins," *Barnes & Noble*

[19] From "Interview with Ellen Hopkins," *Barnes & Noble*

[20] If you take a quick glance at the first few pages of *Crank* you'll see how well she's adapted traditional storytelling to the format. Between pages one and twenty-five we're introduced to what the story is going to be about (the monster), Kristina, her state of mind, her problem, her family, her alter-ego, her situation: who, what, where, when, why, straight from the heart of this journalist/poet.

story in verse is *hugely* difficult.[21] It's not just a series of linked poems or a collection of poetry. It's story, character, action, description and every other element that builds compelling fiction. Go ahead. Try to develop characters and a convincing, flowing, logical plot within verse's restricted design.

It is *design* that most readers notice first about Ellen's work. "I did spend some time creating a unique 'look' for the poetry in my novels, which I want to stand out from the crowd."[22] As an author of fiction, I'm always seeking the right "form" for a story. This is different from plot, which is the arrangement and sequence of events, or style, which has more to do with the author's voice and use of language. Form is more about finding the best structure to "contain" the story, like a uniquely shaped and decorated box, a way for an author to "own" her work.

The broadest and most obvious example of form and structure in either a prose or verse novel is in the length of a book. Other examples can also be found within the shape of the narrative, in patterns of flashback or shifting points of view, in an author's choice of chapter length or whether to use chapters at all. In Ellen's case, beyond the length of her books and her primary choice to structure Kristina's story in verse, the signature mirror poems that run parallel to the main text, as well as the use of first lines as headings, are

---

[21] The focus is sometimes painfully tight. Choices can be overwhelming: How do you keep the flow of the story action moving forward? How do you hang onto continuity? How do you keep from writing "poems" that don't fit? What about consistency and choosing which scenes to dramatize, which to narrate?
[22] From "Interview with Ellen Hopkins," *Barnes & Noble*

examples of form that make her work stand out from other novels written in verse.

While some reviewers have praised Ellen's verse as "hypnotic"[23] and "masterpieces of word, shape, and pacing,"[24] critics of novels written in verse often begin their arguments with the suggestion that the poetry amounts to nothing more than prose broken into stanzas,[25] adding that most line breaks are arbitrary, convenient, and artificial, and that there is nothing necessarily "poetic" about them. I'm not certain if anyone has come up with a clear definition of a verse novel. I've heard editors refer to the line breaks as "natural speaking phrases" that set a rhythm of speech in the reader's mind. But a close inspection of the formatting in *Crank* and *Glass* reveals much more than just a broken line. Take a look at the work "shape" does in these books. It not only echoes content, it also adds impact by inviting a second reading,[26] creating expectations and surprises, increasing tension and tug, adding emotional weight, speeding up action, and deepening characterization.

Ellen has used verse format to her advantage in other ways, as well. Her clever use of first-line banners, sometimes as titles, sometimes as part of the following section of verse, gives readers a heads up, acting as single-line transitions between place, situation, or as

---

[23] *Kirkus* book review of *Crank* (taken from the Barnes & Noble page)

[24] *School Library Journal* book review of *Crank* (taken from the Barnes & Noble page)

[25] For a scathing review of Ellen's verse format, visit http://cesario.blogspot.com/2006/09/burned-by-ellen-hopkins.html. Make sure to read the comments, as well.

[26] In which you might find a secondary or even "hidden" meaning.

subliminal invitations for the reader to keep going, effectively and efficiently hooking readers into the next poetic section.[27]

The simple way she's formatted dialogue in italics without using tags (he said/she said) gives readers an unbroken connection to Kristina's thoughts. As you read, it's as if you are listening to what's being said to Kristina as *Kristina* hears it. This works in part because Ellen has used verse format to set off what's being said to Kristina, adding a visual separation between the characters. It also works because Kristina's reaction, whether said aloud or processed internally, comes immediately, without any technical interruption.

In all things, Ellen is about brevity—brevity born from the poet she is at heart. "I like having every word count. I like not having to do pages of description if a sentence will do. That spareness increases the power of the language."[28] And the language *is* powerful. The *poetry* is powerful. The first time I read *Crank* and then again when I read *Glass*, I remember being struck by an almost irresistible urge to shout, "Come! Look at this! See what I've found! Check out this evocative shape, this example of figurative language, this exquisite word choice!" I wanted to reach out, grab someone, point to every subtle double entendre, clever allusion, turn of phrase, touch of humor, tone of voice, internal rhyme, assonance, and on and on. Oh, yes. They are all there, literary devices Mary Oliver, Babette

---

[27] See *Crank*, p. 226 that begins "As I Pondered" and read through the next few to find headings that brilliantly act as setting, transitions, and leads.
[28] From "Ellen Hopkins" in *Publishers Weekly*'s Children's Bookshelf

Deutsch, and Judson Jerome call to attention in their handbooks on poetry.[29]

Verse format and *poetry* have given Kristina an honest, original voice that plays more like music than simple "natural speaking phrases." Kristina's voice is an invitation that acts as a direct conduit between Ellen and her readers.[30] But unlike many of today's young adult novels, these books do not depend on cookie cutter teen voices rife with gratuitous contemporary slang created by an author trying to sound current or trying to make her characters sound current. Take a look at word choices such as: *assuaged, trepidation, hierarchy, inextricable, tempestuous, resplendent,* and *exponentially.* Exactly whose vocabulary is this? A typical teenager's? Not really. The heart of it belongs to Ellen. This is also evident in the occasional touches of flowery language that some critics have referred to as overreaching

---

[29] By the time I finished re-reading *Crank* and *Glass* in preparation for this essay, each of the books were decorated with a bright parade of post-its marking the discoveries I wanted to share, obviously impossible to do in these few pages. But open either book at random. You'll be surprised at what you'll find once you start looking. For example, check out "Choices, Choices" on p. 83 of *Crank* for some great examples of assonance. *Assonance* is the repetition or similarity of two or more vowel sounds within a line or verse. It and it's consonant partner, consonance, play a huge part in creating the rhythms within Ellen's verse.

[30] As posts made to Ellen's MySpace and online message boards testify, over and over again. For example, this post from Stephanie: "*Crank* is an AMAZING book! This is the only book I have ever read that made me feel the character's emotion and made me feel like that person." And from Jessica: "I felt like I myself had become what Kristina was and one night my mother stormed into my room and my first thought was, 'She knows what I've been doing!' But when I went, wait a minute, that's not me at all! Very bizarre." From Ellen's message board: http://www.allreaders.com/board.asp?listpage=2&boardid=32151.

lines.[31] To a critical eye they may seem "out of step," but in choosing the language of poetry Ellen has allowed herself to remain true to her poetic sensibilities. And by not dumbing down the language, she's shown respect for the intelligence of her readers. Neither poet nor reader has been short-changed. Once again, by being true to herself, Ellen has made the connection.

Some believe Ellen was "definitely on a mission"[32] when she chose to connect with this audience, that her motivation for writing *Crank* and *Glass* was to warn young readers of the tragedy of addiction. Yes (well, duh), that is what the story is about, after all. But I don't believe she was ever[33] on a mission to preach or teach a behavioral lesson to young readers, as some have implied. Certainly, thoughts of "should do this" and "shouldn't do that" do cross Kristina's mind more than once as she makes decisions, and are likely echoed by readers as they walk with her through each of her choices and mistakes. Yet at no time does Ellen set Kristina up as a tragic heroine acting out a moral lesson in a classic cautionary tale. In fact, the only obviously intentional lesson in these books is more about how the *drug* behaves than about how Kristina behaves. Though she is certainly flawed,[34] in no way are her flaws particular

---

[31] "A few overreaching lines seem out of step with character voices: a boyfriend, for example, tells Kristina that he'd like to wait for sex until she is 'free from dreams of yesterday.'" From Gillian Engberg's "*Review of Crank*" in *Booklist Magazine* (taken from the Amazon.com page).

[32] *Publisher's Weekly* book review (taken from the Amazon.com page)

[33] . . . or has ever been . . .

[34] A condition of being human, right? And according to Aristotle, a necessity for creating a strong plot.

to her or written into the story as an illustration of anything other than her ordinariness. In turn, by making Kristina "an ordinary girl," she was able to address the real horror of addiction—that it can happen to *anyone,* and not because a person is "bad," a victim, or a fool. Kristina Georgia Snow is no Hardy's Tess, or Flaubert's Emma, or Mitchell's Scarlett. Her story may be tragic, but she is no more a tragic heroine than any other kid out there trying to navigate our modern world. For me, this is clear evidence that if Ellen was on any mission, it was fundamentally a mission to connect with her readers.

For many of us, connection is why we *must* write in the first place. As children, we want to connect. We tug on someone's sleeve to show them what we've found, what we know, what we've done. *Notice me. Share this moment with me. Come into my world.* That urge does not go away as we grow up. But there's more to it than that . . .

It's about making art. Some say that "close witness of the world . . . is the beginning of art."[35] I would add that hand-in-hand with this beginning comes the *desire to create,* a desire that's been planted in our genes for thousands of years. Witness ancient man/woman and their desire to leave marks on the walls of their caves. Was their impulse to draw born of a longing for control, a longing to make something out of nothing, to make the world a better place? Or were they drawing to illustrate events, leave records, or just get something off their minds? To understand? Tell stories? Make prayers? Maybe

---

[35] Kim R. Stafford in *The Muses among Us: Eloquent Listening and Other Pleasures of the Writer's Craft*

they were on a mission to teach or preach.[36] We probably will never know, but no matter the specific reason, I believe the compulsion to *share an experience* is driven by a common deep desire—the *need* to connect.[37] And in my mind, this instinctive need must be related to the urge to put the world into words in order to share it, born in us along with the desire to shout out, "Come! Look at this! See what I've found!" that rests solidly in our awareness that we are part of a community. In my mind, the desire to create *is* the desire to connect. And the desire to connect is a necessity, because connection has always been about survival.

Bill Moyers has said that "Connecting is crucial to being a poet."[38] For a poet-turned-novelist like Ellen this couldn't be more true. Behind each of her writing choices one senses a writer working to break through barriers. A mother who has exhausted possibilities. Someone longing to connect with readers in ways she was unable to ever connect with her own daughter after that daughter met the monster. And she *has* made that connection—with a huge number of readers—readers who know she will tell them the truth . . . and not just because she takes honesty, herself, and her readers seriously enough to post her true age on her website.

---

[36] Of course, the baser side of me does wonder if these ancient artists were forced to draw or possibly rewarded for their efforts with an extra drumstick or tenderloin.

[37] I'm stopping myself from being sidetracked by an obvious question: Is the prevalence of graffiti (and other "bad behavior") directly linked to the lack of art in our schools?

[38] Bill Moyers' introduction to *The Language of Life, A Festival of Poets*

So, who are these readers? A review of Ellen's MySpace and Facebook pages makes it obvious that the mainstay of her readership is not made up only of addicts or lost souls. Yes, many of her readers are troubled, many are abused. But many are "good," "normal," even "above average" kids, just like Kristina before she met the monster. What do they have in common? They're all hungering for the same thing: connection, knowing someone out there "gets it." In Ellen's eyes:

> My core readership is this wonderful generation of teens that is honest and hopeful . . . But they also have had all these difficult experiences in their lives. . . . I hope I can show them a way past the black moments, show them that there are people around them that care. Often they get this feeling that "It's just me against the world, nobody cares about me." If I can help them see the connections in their own lives to friends or family, or a way past their addiction, or a way past cutting, or a way past these thoughts of ending it all, that's more important than anything.[39]

But to make these connections must a writer pretend to be someone she's not? Must she sacrifice her creative vision, her writing sensibilities, and who she really is in order to gather an audience and give birth to a bestseller? No, I don't think so. In fact, by being true to herself as a writer, Ellen has in turn been true to her readers, and connected with them *through* rather than *in spite of* who she is. And

---

[39] From "Ellen Hopkins" in *Publishers Weekly*'s Children's Bookshelf

the way I look at it, this is another deeper message readers can take away from her books, isn't it? *Be true to who you are—no matter who you are. Choose yourself. Respect yourself.* I marvel at the way Ellen has said this, without preaching or teaching, and without actually ever saying it on the page.

Of course, someone else said it ages ago, which is as it is with most "truths":

> This above all: to thine own self be true,
> And it must follow, as the night the day,
> Thou canst not then be false to any man. (*Hamlet*)

Okay, I apologize. Shakespeare might be a cheap shot, but sometimes I just can't help myself. Those three lines pretty much spell out everything it's taken me these dozen or so pages to say, and they seem a tidy summary to help send you off on the right track—him being a bestselling poet, and all.

Susan Hart Lindquist is a graduate of the University of California, Santa Barbara, an award-winning poet, and the author of three novels for young readers (*Summer Soldiers*, *Wander*, and *Walking the Rim*). In the field of children's poetry she has had works published in anthologies (*Oh, No! Where Are my Pants!* and *Climb Into My Lap*), both compiled by Lee Bennett Hopkins. Currently, she is writing fiction for young adults and learning to paint, play the violin, and live on a ranch a million miles from nowhere.

Love is an elixir,
so poets claim, a frothy hormonal
brew to cure what's ailing you. Drink
it in. Sip it slowly. Savor
its peculiar flavor as loneliness
and pain all melt away.

Dive headlong into the rush,
ride the raging river up against
the brink, careful not to drown. Drop
over the edge. Negotiate your fall,
for drug or love or object thrown,
one thing is certain. What goes up
eventually comes down.

Poets and songwriters have long been fascinated by the concept of love as a drug—an addiction many people actively seek out and engage in, often to an unhealthy degree. Now some scientists agree it's possible, having found compelling evidence that a certain chemical in the brain might be responsible for all addictions. What do drugs and love have in common? And what did that mean for Kristina? Megan Kelley Hall explains.

Love Is an Addiction

Megan Kelley Hall

When one is in love, one always begins by deceiving oneself, and one always ends by deceiving others. That is what the world calls a romance.

—OSCAR WILDE

Everyone knows the urgency, the importance, and the agony of love. In the first throws of love you can't eat, you can't sleep, your heart and mind race, and you are completely consumed. You experience your highest highs and lowest lows. You don't always think rationally. You constantly crave your next fix.

Wait, what are we talking about again? Oh right, love. Funny, it also sounds an awful lot like addiction.

People have been comparing love and addiction for decades. It's an idea that shows up especially often in song lyrics. In 1985, Robert Palmer sang, "You might as well face it you're addicted to love." In 1976, Roxy Music wrote, "Love is the drug." The lyrics to Kelly Clarkson's 2004 song "Addicted" illustrate the similarities between being addicted to someone and just being an addict:

> It's like you're a drug
> It's like you're a demon I can't face down . . .
> I'm addicted to you

The infatuation, the euphoria, the excitement—it can all be attributed to love or to drugs. Kristina Snow can tell you that better than most.

Kristina, the protagonist in Ellen Hopkins' bestselling books *Crank* and *Glass*, is a girl who is familiar with both. For Kristina, the two not only have a lot in common, they are actually linked.

Kristina gets her first taste of both love and the drug she becomes addicted to at the same time, thanks to the same guy: Adam, a.k.a. Buddy. It's her desire for love and acceptance, from both Buddy and her father, that drives her to try the drug for the first time. When she gets back home, relationships with guys is how she obtains drugs, and the context in which she usually uses them. It's no wonder love and drugs soon become an interchangeable addiction.

Love Is an Addiction

Even before the summer we meet her, Kristina Snow is desperate for love. She feels abandoned by everyone: her mother, her junkie father, her older sister. Her desperation to feel loved leads her down a path of drugs, sex, secrets, and lies; it's why she wants to visit her father in the first place.

This desperation is a hole in her heart that she tries to fill with drugs. But the more drugs she takes, the larger the hole that needs to be filled. It becomes a never-ending cycle as she tries to meet her need for one by using the other. Kristina's love for her baby almost substitutes for her addiction to drugs, but as soon as she's feeling like she needs a guy again, she starts feeling like she needs to use again, too.

> I needed
> Adam,
> his heart,
> his promises,
> his tomorrows. . . .
>
> I needed
> my mommy.
>
> And all that made me really
> really need
>
> a line.

It's a downward spiral from that point on.

Recent studies show that the difference between drugs and love isn't actually that big. Researchers have discovered that the emotions of love actually trigger the same parts of the brain that are affected by drugs.

Helen E. Fisher, Ph.D., a professor of anthropology at Rutgers University and author of *Why We Love: The Nature and Chemistry of Romantic Love* researched the addictive nature of love by scanning the brains of people in love and found an amazing correlation. When volunteers were shown pictures of their love interests the areas of the brain that lit up directly corresponded to areas of the brain shown to be affected by drugs. So, essentially, love *is* a drug.

"When I first started looking at the properties of infatuation, they had some of the same elements of a cocaine high: sleeplessness, loss of a sense of time, absolute focus on love to the detriment of all around you," Fisher said of her research when interviewed by *Psychology Today* magazine.

Fisher continued, "It became apparent to me that romantic love was a drive—a drive as strong as thirst, as hunger. People live for love, they kill for love, they die for love, they sing about love."

But love is supposed to be a good thing, right? Love helps you grow and improve every part of your life. It benefits your health, your relationships, your very existence. Drugs, on the other hand, rip that life apart.

All of that is true. But love can be dangerous, too. According to *Psychology Today*, people can actually become addicted to high levels of phenylethylamine (PEA), a chemical in the brain that is involved in the euphoria triggered by falling in love. Love, like drugs, can be *literally* addictive. And the problem with addicts, both of love and of drugs, is that they inevitably end up hurting the people around them.

"The easiest definition of addiction is this: an addiction is something we can't stop doing," Joe Dispenza, D.C., explains in his bestselling book *Evolve Your Brain*. "Among its symptoms are lethargy, a lack of ability to focus, a tremendous desire to maintain routine in our daily life, the inability to complete cycles of action, a lack of new experiences and emotional responses, and the persistent feeling that one day is the same as the next and the next."

He continues by explaining that "almost all thoughts are emotionally based, and when we recall them, we are also associating the emotions stored with them. . . . Once activated, that frame of mind produces a plethora of chemicals, both in the synaptic space and from the mid-brain's hypothalamus, to stimulate the brain and body. Each thought has its own chemical signature. The result is that our thinking becomes feeling—actually our every thought is a feeling." And when it comes to emotional addicts, they can't get enough of that feeling. They are dependent upon the physical and psychological arousal being in love triggers.

Susan Cheever, author and daughter of the famous writer John Cheever, writes about her own battles with sexual addiction and recounts tales of other love addicts in the book *Desire: Where Sex Meets Addiction*. In an interview in the *New York Times*, Cheever admitted, "It's only in writing this book that I've come to see that all addictions are one addiction, which is the most interesting idea in the book. Addiction isn't about substance—you aren't addicted to the substance, you are addicted to the alteration of mood that the substance brings. And if that substance is taken away, you'll replace it with another substance." Kristina's tendency to swap drugs for love, and vice versa, isn't that far from reality after all.

Some of the same technique used by people in 12-step programs to get over drug and alcohol addictions are often prescribed for those suffering from a broken heart or lost love. For example, psychologist and certified sexual addiction specialist Brenda Schaeffer, author of *Is it Love or Is It Addiction?*, outlines the following steps to help people forget the past and focus on the future, and thereby break the cycle of addiction:

- Assess yourself for love addiction tendencies honestly. Some signs include obsessive thoughts about another person that interfere with your life and feelings of worthlessness or depression when not in a relationship.
- Be willing to face the pain letting go produces.
- Discover and address the underlying causes and psychological beliefs that support the compulsive/obsessive behavior. Ask yourself questions like, "What do I believe about relationships, love, and myself? Why might I fear closeness? Do I believe people will disappoint me or I will disappoint them?"
- Don't forget the past; use it. Acknowledge that you will move beyond any painful experiences and focus on a better future.
- Find a support group to help you through this transition.

And if you compare the 12-step program to help people addicted to drugs and alcohol to the 12-step program to help people with emotional addiction, you'll find that they are identical.

Obsession with love and drugs is timeless, and Kristina's is a struggle that has gone on for ages. Kristina's bad-boy boyfriend Chase (who turns out to be her white knight), quotes the eighteenth century poet John Keats as they indulge together:

> Give me women, wine, and snuff
> Until I cry out hold, enough!
> You may do so sans objection
> Till the day of resurrection; for
> Bless my beard they aye shall be
> My beloved Trinity.

Unfortunately, in all these centuries, no one's yet found a cure.

The 12 Steps of Crystal Meth Anonymous

1. We admitted that we were powerless over **crystal meth** and our lives had become unmanageable.
2. Came to believe that a power greater than ourselves could restore us to sanity.

continued on next page

The 12 Steps of Crystal Meth Anonymous, *continued*

3. Made a decision to turn our will and our lives over to the care of a God of our understanding.

4. Made a searching and fearless moral inventory of ourselves.

5. Admitted to God, to ourselves, and to another human being the exact nature of our wrongs.

6. Were entirely ready to have God remove all these defects of character.

7. Humbly asked God to remove our shortcomings.

8. Made a list of all persons we had harmed and became willing to make amends to them all.

9. Made direct amends to such people wherever possible, except when to do so would injure them or others.

10. Continued to take personal inventory and when we were wrong promptly admitted it.

11. Sought through prayer and meditation to improve our conscious contact with a God of our understanding praying only for the knowledge of God's will for us, and the power to carry that out.

12. Having had a spiritual awakening as a result of these steps, we tried to carry this message to **crystal meth addicts**, and to practice these principles in all of our affairs.

REPRINTED BY PERMISSION OF A.A. WORLD SERVICES, INC.

The 12 Steps of Sex
and Love Addicts Anonymous

1. We admitted we were powerless over **sex and love** addiction—that our lives had become unmanageable.
2. Came to believe that a Power greater than ourselves could restore us to sanity.
3. Made a decision to turn our will and our lives over to the care of God as we understood God.
4. Made a searching and fearless moral inventory of ourselves.
5. Admitted to God, to ourselves, and to another human being the exact nature of our wrongs.
6. Were entirely ready to have God remove all these defects of character.
7. Humbly asked God to remove our shortcomings.
8. Made a list of all persons we had harmed, and became willing to make amends to them all.
9. Made direct amends to such people wherever possible, except when to do so would injure them or others.
10. Continued to take personal inventory, and when we were wrong promptly admitted it.
11. Sought through prayer and meditation to improve our conscious contact with a Power greater than ourselves, praying only for knowledge of God's will for us and the power to carry that out.
12. Having had a spiritual awakening as the result of these steps, we tried to carry this message to **sex and love addicts**, and to practice these principles in all areas of our lives.

Megan Kelley Hall is the author of the young adult suspense thriller *Sisters of Misery* (Kensington 2008). Ellen Hopkins praised Hall's debut novel and said, "One of the very best things in life is discovering an author you want to read more of. *Sisters of Misery* makes me want to read a whole lot more of Megan Kelley Hall." The second in the series, *The Lost Sister*, is due out in 2009. Hall lives with her husband and daughter on Boston's North Shore.

We enter this world
with innocent needs.
         Sustenance.
             Shelter.
                 Nurturing.
                 Connection.

We grow, learning through
reward, to want.
         Toys.
             Cars.
                 Money.
                 Connection.

When reward becomes the goal,
want becomes desire.
         Drugs.
             Booze.
                 Sex.
                 Connection.

When desire becomes need,
desperation follows.
         D
             i
                 s
                 connection.

Few of us go through our lives without experiencing addiction, either directly or through someone we care about. Science tells us a person may be predisposed to addiction, and there are high-risk predictors. Yet some who carry them don't become addicted, while others who are free of such predictors fall headlong into addiction. Where, then, does addiction truly begin? Why do some escape it, while others can't pull free? Why do some addicts function fairly well, while others end up in prison, or worse? Counselor Mary Bryan outlines the nature of addiction.

Why Kristina Can't Just Quit

Mary Bryan

Addiction is a puzzle, difficult to understand because it is different in each person. It is a disease of the brain, but it is not just physical. It's also psychological, social, neurological, and environmental. Addiction is not secondary to another condition like a mental health disorder. It is a primary condition; the addictive disease is what causes the drinking and/or drug use, not the other way around.

Some of the predictors of addiction include physical or sexual abuse, family history of substance abuse or alcoholism, depression, anxiety, conduct disturbances, personality disorders, poor coping skills, chaotic living environment, and heavy tobacco use, and one study even mentions previous multiple automobile accidents. But while there are high-risk predictors, many people who have all of them do not become addicts, and people who have none of the predictors do become addicts. No one can predict accurately who will become addicted and who will not.

The Addictive Process

The general pattern of addiction is one of progression. There is no turning back. An addict cannot back up and start over as if they never drank or used drugs before. Even addicts who remained clean for many years report that their behavior became out of control again almost immediately when they returned to drinking or drug use. While there is no simple cure for addiction, it can be treated by behavior changes that remove the addict from the places, people, and activities their brain associates with substance use.

The severity of addiction runs the gamut from minimal to ultimate. In minimal addiction, the addict can still operate in the world. They are generally able to get to work, take care of their children (even if it is with the help of others), pay some of their bills,, rebound from their use of substances enough to be somewhat communicative, and able to avoid having to steal outright to pay for their substance of choice.

This ability to function is particularly true of persons who use stimulants and the depressant alcohol. While using methamphetamine and cocaine, people can remain alert, although they may exhibit moodiness or other personality changes. If they feel themselves beginning to crash, they take another hit. If no drugs are available, huge quantities of caffeine can temporarily stave off the need to sleep. Even though alcohol is a depressant, many alcoholics can operate machinery, work, and interact with people; they build up a remarkable tolerance for the effects. These types of addicts are called functional addicts. Functional addicts may be in the late stage of addiction, but still manage to support themselves and mostly avoid external consequences, like arrests. A functional addict is not the same as a minimal addict. Minimal addicts abuse drugs or alcohol, but have not lost control of their use.

In the early stages of use, a potential addict often tries drugs only socially and in response to peer pressure. Beginning users usually continue to use, however, because the drug allows them to feel like they can leave the pressures of life behind; they may have few other ways of coping with the rough edges of life. At first, they are tentative about using drugs and surprised by the pleasure they get from using. The early-stage addict feels like there is no way the divine reward of the high—the rush of pleasure, the flooding of the reward pathway—can be a bad thing.

Initially, they may hide drug-seeking behavior behind some semblance of normality. Some early-stage addicts for example, may only use with someone else, as if they are just using to be friendly. At this point, the person still has some control over their habits. They may use purposefully, to escape stress and tension, as much as for the high. Then they develop a pattern of use. They begin to use more and more often. Once past the minimal stage, the addict begins to spend more and more time seeking out the substance, using the substance, and recovering from the substance. Use becomes more and more conspicuous. Addicts demonstrate increased tolerance to their drug of choice, and exhibit physical withdrawal symptoms when they go without the substance for any length of time.

Addicts are out of control, but develop incredible reasons, excuses, and alibis to explain their behaviors. They begin to protect their supply and show anti-social behavior. Addicts binge. They need to use just to get up in the morning. They lose touch with their morality.

As the addiction progresses, normal functioning is reduced significantly. Addicts' ability to get to work diminishes—they miss more days and log more late arrivals. The end of the week never comes soon enough, so addicts take off a lot of Fridays or Friday afternoons. Their ability to show up for work on Mondays becomes a crap shoot as well. The addiction and thoughts of using replace most thoughts of normal life: not just going to work, but taking care of children, cooking meals, cleaning the house, engaging in healthy recreation, and many other daily activities. Phone calls from caring people go unreturned unless they pertain to drugs or drug-related activities. Addicts have no time to waste on clean and sober people.

They bring nothing to the late-stage addict that provides pleasure; therefore, they have little value.

Without treatment, addiction generally continues to worsen until the disease results in the addict's death. Even when addicts manage to stop using temporarily, when they begin using again, they pick up right where they left off the last time they used. They can never start over. They never get a clean slate.

Inside the Addict's Head

As minimal abuse progresses to ultimate addiction, a delusional thinking process evolves. This delusion is often believable to both the addict and his or her loved ones. They both think things will get better. They believe that external changes will make the addiction and the desire for the drug go away. They blame the addiction on the addict's job, marriage, stress, or just bad luck. It takes a long time for addicts and their families to realize that the addicts' drug use is entirely responsible for their life difficulties.

The addict fails to stop or reduce the amount of the drugs he or she is using, despite constant verbalization of the desire to do so. Though the addict may repeatedly attempt to control his or her drug use, he or she usually fails. This failure is often a source of persistent remorse, and often drives the addict to avoid family and friends. The addict denies that the drug use is a problem, despite feedback to the contrary from important people in his or her life.

As the addict enters the final phase of addiction, we see moral deterioration and the onset of lengthy intoxication, accompanied by significant impairment of thinking. The ultimate addict is unable to initiate any positive action. The addict is obsessed with the drug use and demonstrates this by viewing everything outside the drug as meaningless. Addiction changes the brain so that no pleasure is possible without the stimulus of the drug chemicals. The addict receives no high or pleasure from the company of others, or from having a clean and tidy place to live. The previously comforting presence of family, friends, and home become painful remembrances that they have to avoid. The addict begins to associate family and friends with negative emotions. And once the pleasure pathways of the brain have become distorted, the only way the addict can "enjoy" themselves, or even just feel normal, is to use and be under the influence.

Drug addicts typically do little but drug seek. They talk about having lives outside of their addiction, but in fact, rarely do. Addicts spend hours justifying their way of living, even as, somewhere deep within, they may feel remorseful and wish that they could have both the drug habit and their life. But given the choice between the drug and their family and job, they choose the drug—because there really is no choice for them. Their brain has changed. The addict's only path is the one that takes him or her to the easy reward: the chemical stimulus of their drug of choice.

Addicts are frequently underemployed or unemployed due to their addictive behavior but usually fail to see the connection. If the addict works, they frequently work with other drug users who support their addiction. For these addicts, recovery is difficult. Even admitting they have a problem can be impossible: sometimes addicts can delude themselves into thinking they are alright since there are other people around them who are much worse off. And an addict will often insist his or her addiction is under control even as they suffer from withdrawal symptoms, and other negative consequences of addiction like loss of family and homelessness. Eventually, the addict is financially destitute. He or she usually lives with other drug users, which creates an environment in which the addict is at high risk of relapse even if he or she did manage to stop using.

Though the hallmarks of addiction I've described here occur in most addicts, this addictive process is not the same for everyone. The unpredictability of addiction is what is so frightening. In a group of three friends, two people might use a drug socially and minimally, while the third person becomes an out-of-control "ultimate" addict within a few very short weeks. The combination of personality traits, genetic make-up, stress level, thinking patterns, environment, and other high-risk factors that contribute to addiction make it unpredictable. Let's look at one example and how her addiction fits into this pattern: Kristina Snow.

Methamphetamine and Kristina Snow

Methamphetamine, or meth, is a stimulant that works in a specific way in the brain. It forces the release of a chemical, dopamine, that creates the high. Then, the meth blocks the re-absorption of this chemical, allowing to increase, accumulate, and continue to stimulate the user for much longer than cocaine. The longer you use, the harder it is for your body to manufacture this chemical naturally, without meth. Studies show that users can feel depressed for three to six months after they stop using, until the body's ability to produce dopamine returns. Long-term meth use alters your brain chemistry, causing the cravings for the drug to increase. Typically, ultimate meth addicts relapse numerous times before achieving sobriety.

Meth addiction leads to sleep deprivation, loss of appetite, escalated heart rate, blood pressure elevation, severe malnutrition, dental deterioration, irritability, paranoia, anxiety, aggression, mental confusion, poor judgment, impaired memory, and depression. Meth also increases your risk for HIV and hepatitis B and C. A meth overdose can even cause convulsions, stroke, hyperthermia, and premature delivery of babies.

One of the biggest differences between users addicted to meth and those addicted to depressants like alcohol, heroin, and oxycontin is that meth addicts are awake all the time. The depressants put people to sleep or cause them to "nod off" into a state of semiconsciousness. Being awake for long periods of time causes distortions in your thinking and an unrealistic perception of your surroundings. Staying awake increases the consumption of the drug because of the long span of time available; depressant addicts have to wait for their drug's effects to wear off before they can use more. Staying awake also means the addict has many more hours available for theft, drug-seeking, and other negative behaviors.

Kristina Snow seems set up for addiction from the first time we meet her. It is as if she was only waiting for the right drug to come along. Kristina seems to have the early thoughts and feelings of an addict even before she tries meth for the first time. Sometimes addicts say they never really felt like they fit in or were like other people. They report having felt "less than" or unable to be normal, and when they started drinking or using drugs, they felt normal for the first time. Kristina felt more comfortable as Bree than she did all those years as the "perfect" daughter. Some people believe that this feeling of not being normal is something that, in addicts, was always there, and always will be there.

Also, Kristina's dad has his own addictive disorder, which gives her a clear family history of addiction (he spends all his rent money on drugs, which indicates he is in a fairly advanced stage of addiction). Kristina becomes addicted to meth rapidly; she spends only three weeks with her dad, but by the time she returns to her mom's house, she is hooked. On the plane ride back she realizes that her need for the drug has caused her beautiful home and comfortable mattress to lose all importance to her. Barring forceful intervention, her downfall is already inevitable.

Kristina recognizes that meth is hard on her body but the high is so great that she believes it is worth it. She notices that she isn't interested in food, can't sleep, and knows she will crash, but still "invites the demons in." She understands that her behavior is crazy, but she can't stop herself. She acknowledges that, though the drugs make her fly, they also make her unable to turn back. Bree says meth "launched me to a place very near the gates of heaven." She thinks of meth as something she uses because she wants to (she uses it only because she chooses to), but at other times, she notes that she "needs" meth just to get through a day. In the very early days, she doesn't worry about consequences, and says, "I don't give a damn."

Kristina rapidly sheds her normal morality. She steals from her mother because her mother won't find out about it for a while. She begins to lie to obtain access to the drug and avoid having to be sober. Kristina still has some control, but it is clear that Bree, the ultimate addict, is wide-awake and starting to take over. She talks about having a completely new sense of self. Even before she reaches the ultimate addict stage, "Kristina" is already gone.

The rush of being bad encourages Kristina to take more chances. She becomes less and less able to track her surroundings and the reactions of others. She demonstrates more and more disrespect, openly disobeying her parents instead of trying to hide her actions. She also takes more and more chances with her body, moving from snorting to smoking, and participating in sexual activities with no protection.

Her drug use leads to a new set of friends, dealers and other users. All her old non-using friends have become useless, and she quickly loses touch with them. She makes frequent promises to herself to moderate her use or to stop completely. All these promises fail. The intensity of her need for the drug takes her breath away, and occasionally she even sees it as "grasping" at her.

The consequences continue to increase in severity. She fails school, owes lots of money, piles lies upon lies, and disregards her deteriorating health. She steals, deals, and becomes pregnant. She cannot stop completely even when pregnant. She cannot stay off nicotine either.

She becomes self-involved and allows her ego to rule her personality. She cannot stop using and does not want to. She casts aside offers of help with ridicule. Not a day passes that she doesn't think about getting high. After temporarily stopping the drug use while pregnant, she justifies using again by rationalizing that it will help her lose her baby weight and stay awake to take care of her baby. An immediate return to addictive use follows.

Kristina's downward spiral in *Glass* shows her physical deterioration: weight loss, sores on her face, dingy hair, chipped teeth, and bleeding gums. She describes a tortured emotional and psychological life. She loses her friends and family members, and replaces them all with addicts and dealers. She starts out living in a beautiful home in the Valley and ends up sleeping in her car, living in motels, or crashing in other people's homes.

Is There Hope for Kristina?

Addiction can be arrested if alcohol or drug use ends. The brain and body chemistry can return to relatively normal functioning given enough time, allowing the addict to lead a normal life—*if* they can achieve and maintain sobriety. Denial and relapse happen frequently.

Meth addiction is a particularly difficult disorder to work with, but it is not impossible. Addicts often appear to have a personality disorder, due to a high incidence of impulsive, irrational, and sometimes paranoid behaviors. Treatment for methamphetamine abuse or dependence parallels the treatment for a broken bone; treatment provides the structure, like a cast, which allows the body time to heal itself. In the case of meth addiction, the brain's chemistry is out of tune and takes a while to recover. Treatment "immobilizes" the meth addict, preventing him or her from making foolish and impulsive decisions while the brain is not at its best operationally. The treatment team oversees what the addict does, when the addict does it, and how the addict does it. The team guides the addict to avoid dangerous places like bars, meth addicts' homes, and other places where drugs are readily available, in addition old friends who use. As the meth addict remains in recovery, the brain begins to function better and the oversight of the treatment team decreases proportionately.

The studies that have been done with meth addicts show a few milestones of sobriety. Ninety days of sobriety are necessary to clear the primary dysfunctional thinking. Addicts most commonly relapse within six months, because their brains are producing abnormally low levels of dopamine and they cannot experience pleasure without the drug. Studies show about 50 to 60 percent of addicts remain drug free at the end of one year, but it takes two years of sobriety for the body to complete the first wave of chemical and psychological repair. Overall, the recovery rate for meth addicts is higher than that of heroin addicts, but not as good as that of alcoholics.

Successful treatment should last at least nine months (though two years is optimum) to reset the cognitive behavioral thinking processes and include a minimum of three groups per week for the first ninety days. Throughout the recovery process, the addict should receive coaching from a professional who supplies encouragement and assistance as the addict changes his or her lifestyle:

budgets resources, sets goals and creates realistic plans to achieve them, builds a safety net of friends and acquaintances, and develops work skills and good work practices.

The treatment plan should employ specific methods to re-introduce natural pleasures. Addicts need addiction education in things like craving management and avoidance of risky activities like drinking alcohol. Relapse prevention counseling, as well as full-time work focusing on rebuilding family ties and the addict's financial situation, is particularly important. Regular urine testing throughout treatment is helpful because it keeps the addict accountable for his or her behavior. He or she should also become involved in the self-help community; this is how members of 12-step programs like Alcoholics Anonymous refer to themselves. The addict should begin his or her twelve steps and complete through step four prior to finishing the treatment program. As part of their treatment planning, the addict must also acquire a sponsor.

Certain prescription medication can also be employed to excellent effect. The use of Zyban or Welbutrin as an antidepressant should begin early, if necessary. The anti-nausea drug Zofran, which has been shown to work against relapse with alcoholics, might be tried in certain circumstances. The Prometa method (a private, for-profit system that infuses recovering addicts with certain chemicals to help them through withdrawal) may be useful in very early recovery, but must be followed with the twelve to eighteen months of cognitive behavioral treatment.

Research shows that the use of cognitive behavioral therapy (CBT) can be extremely helpful independent of the Prometa method as well. In fact, many people consider CBT to be one of the best ways of treating substance abusers. CBT is based on the idea that our thoughts are the cause of certain feelings and behaviors—that it is negative thought processes that cause us to feel certain ways, not external things like people, situations, and events. Therefore, we can change the way we feel about a situation by changing the way we think, even if the situation itself remains the same. CBT therapists believe that clients change because they learn how to think differently. CBT therapists focus on teaching "rational self-talk" skills: replacing negative thoughts like "I will never be able to stop using" with positive thoughts focusing on their sobriety goals ("I can stop using by asking for support from my family").

If Kristina were to begin treatment, she would be expected to maintain custody of her children, to hold down a job, and to work on developing healthy family relationships. And with the help of regular counseling and the support of her family and of other women in recovery from similar addictions, Kristina has a strong chance of remaining sober for the long-term, and getting her life back.

Mary Bryan has a masters in psychology, and has been directly involved with alcohol and drug treatment for the last twenty-eight years. For the past twenty years, she's been the director of the Community Counseling Center, a non-profit substance treatment facility with an outpatient building and a thirty-two-bed joint commission accredited residential facility for alcohol and drug treatment, in Carson City, Nevada

The monster is a hydra,
a multi-headed beast,

                              voracious

in its appetites. One taste,
he wants the rest,
nothing left but bones.

                              Rapacious.

Close your ears to his
patient invitation, his gentle
hiss a serenaded

                              serpent

song. Beware the deep
clear of his eyes, the promises
mirrored there masqueraded

                              lies.

Take care where you step.
For though the monster coils

                              in wait,

the path you negotiate
is yours to choose.

Crystal meth is, indeed, a monster. Once you choose to walk with it—and the choice is all yours to make—you can't easily leave it behind. Judge John Tatro sees the monster's destruction in his courtroom, and the debris belongs not only to the user, but to those who care for him and her. Parents. Children. Siblings. Friends. And in a larger sense, the community that loses a productive, vital member to meth addiction. So, says Tatro, the community must play a role in halting the monster, hopefully before it gains a strong foothold within it.

A View From the Bench

Judge John Tatro

I've been a judge for fourteen years and I've presided over both civil and criminal cases. Since I started, I have seen the number of methamphetamine-related criminal cases rise dramatically. In the beginning, I would see one or two cases a month. Now, there isn't a day that goes by when I'm not dealing with at least one person, typically between eighteen and twenty-five years old, who is addicted to methamphetamine.

As a judge, I have attended many educational seminars dealing with methamphetamine and meth's extremely addictive qualities. I have learned that meth is so powerful many young people become addicted the very first time they use. I have learned that meth causes damage in the user's brain that is extremely difficult to repair, and affects the nervous system. People who use meth develop sores all over their bodies. It also causes their teeth to rot or turn black, and sometimes even fall out. Users lose dramatic amounts of weight and become extremely paranoid.

I also learned why, with all these horrific side effects, people still continued to use meth. A chemical in the brain called dopamine is released whenever a person experiences something pleasant. Dopamine causes the brain to send feelings of pleasure to the mind and body, and the pleasure you experience directly corresponds to the amount of dopamine your brain releases. When you eat your favorite food, 150 dopamine units are released. When you have sex, 200 dopamine units are released. But when you use methamphetamine, 1050 dopamine units are released—five times more dopamine than is released during sex. Even cocaine use only releases 340 units.

This explains how and why people become addicted. However, in all the seminars I attended on meth, I still did not learn what it is like to become addicted and then live with that addiction. *Crank* and *Glass* helped me understand the personal side of meth addiction. In these books, Ellen Hopkins allowed me inside the head of a meth addict, and let me experience how a person, a child, falls prey to the "monster" of meth addiction.

Knowing how and why a person becomes addicted to meth, as well as understanding the destructive power of the drug, is very important and helpful for a judge. But the insight provided in *Crank* and *Glass* may be even more valuable. Knowing how a young addict thinks and unfortunately deceives is powerful. A great example of this is Kristina and her alter ego Bree. Kristina is child-like and innocent. Bree is the tough, fearless, uninhibited thrill seeker who lies just beneath the surface. As a judge, being aware that this duality can and does occur in addicts is a great tool. On many occasions, the police, the prosecutors, and I have been fooled by addicts who appear child-like and innocent and so failed to impose the appropriate sentence to help them address their addiction. Many times the Kristina-types minimize their involvement or blame others for their acts. Sometimes they are very convincing, and because of their age, lack of record, and seemingly innocent ways, it's easy to give them the benefit of the doubt. However, knowing they might have a Bree on board prompts me to not be quite so trusting and to take steps to verify their stories. Many steps are available but the most telling is a drug test. It's nearly impossible for even the most skilled Kristina to talk her way out of a positive urine test. Being able to tell a young person that I know he or she is lying and I have proof to back it up takes away the user's ability to convince me that he or she doesn't have a problem. And once a person admits he or she is addicted, especially in open court, that person has taken the first step toward recovery.

Flirtin' with the Monster

As a judge, one of the most difficult things I do is watch a young person become addicted to meth, or any drug for that matter. I have seen many young adults come to court for the first time looking and acting like Kristina. The first time I see a meth user in court, he or she usually has been arrested for a fairly minor charge, like shoplifting or possession of drug paraphernalia. The person is nervous and afraid about what is going to happen to them. At the first court appearance, he or she still has that young innocent look, is oftentimes crying, and has a genuine fear of court as well as jail. Then, as the months and years progress and as the arrests and court appearances occur more frequently, I see the deterioration taking place. I have seen numerous young people's lives ended by methamphetamine. Several young women I had dealt with in court were found dead because the monster had ravaged their bodies. They died not from a single overdose but instead from constant long-term use.

Meth contains some of the same chemicals that are used to clean out drains and kill rodents. The damage that meth does is devastating and happens quickly. So when I have a young meth user appearing in front of me, I know I need to act fast and make difficult decisions that could possibly save that user's life.

In *Crank*, Kristina uses the "monster" over an extended period of time without being detected, which allows her addiction to completely consume her. This is exactly why I feel it is extremely important to intervene immediately. Once meth use is confirmed—and it is appropriate in the legal process—I sentence the meth user and impose strict conditions. A typical meth-related sentence includes formal probation that includes regular search for (and, if necessary, seizure of) drugs and alcohol, substance abuse counseling, and random drug testing. The probation starts out with strict rules and numerous home visits. Home visits are essential in stopping drug use. It is relatively easy for a person on probation to "clean up" before he or she has a scheduled office visit with a probation officer. However, when that same probation officer conducts a surprise home visit, the results can be very different. Many people don't think the officer will ever come to their homes, and so continue to live destructive lifestyles. It is very common for someone on probation to be arrested for using meth shortly after he or she is sentenced. After a week or two in jail for this first violation, he or she realizes that the sentence is serious. The first violation can be pivotal. Many times people in probation truly realize that they are going to have to get clean and sober if they want to stay out of jail. It's a great opportunity to get young abusers into counseling.

The important fact to remember is that, with counseling, people *can* get clean and sober. Methamphetamine addiction typically requires about eighteen months of intensive counseling. The good news is that, if people complete the eighteen months, they have approximately an 85 percent chance of staying clean. The bad news is that a significant portion do not complete the counseling and end up using again. When I see a young person fail, I know that I cannot give up. I always try to get him or her through the counseling. It may be that he or she has to spend some time in jail between failed counseling attempts, but at least in jail that person is relatively safe and not using meth.

Flirtin' with the Monster

A huge stumbling block for any addict's sobriety is his or her continued association with people who use. These people often include friends and family members. In *Crank* and *Glass*, Kristina's father was responsible for her introduction to meth and used with her on numerous occasions. Her father's addiction blinded him to the fact he was ruining his daughter's life. This phenomenon is extremely offensive but not at all uncommon. Most parents would never dream of giving their children something that changes their lives in such a devastating and fatal way. However, I see many families that include three and even four generations of addicts. I recently had an eighteen-year-old girl in court who had been arrested for stealing items from a retail store, which she planned to sell and then use the money to buy methamphetamine. The girl had not finished high school, and was unemployed and homeless. When she came to court her mom was in the audience. At first my heart went out to her mom, as I thought seeing her young child in jail garb and wearing shackles would be more than most moms could handle. However, I quickly realized mom was not there to support her daughter but instead to find out if her daughter had any money to give her. As soon as mom spoke, I remembered her from a prior case where she had forged checks to get money for meth.

Many families are devastated by methamphetamine addiction. In *Glass*, Kristina chooses meth over her child. I have seen this happen in hundreds of cases. I recall a case where a woman in her late thirties was addicted to meth. She had three children, one of whom was a sophomore in high school. The woman was not working because of her addiction and was having trouble affording meth, so she decided that her sixteen-year-old son would have to finance her lifestyle. The son was playing football in high school and maintaining a C-average—quite an accomplishment for someone so young with such a dysfunctional home life. Mom was desperate though, so she ordered her son to quit school and get a full-time job. The boy did as his mother said and gained employment to pay mom's rent and provide funds for meth. The amazing part of this story is that the young man, with encouragement from the local Boys & Girls Club, eventually returned to school and actually graduated.

Several years ago, I sent a father and son to jail for meth-related crimes. Their cases were unrelated but they ended up in the same cellblock for a little over a month. If I got in trouble with the law, I would be humiliated if my sons or daughter ever found out. I would do everything in my power to shelter them from knowing. But when dad came to court, he told me it was great serving time together. The father and son were able to bond as cellmates. The son, I am told, got in a fight with another inmate over what program to watch on the television, and Dad was proud his son had stood up for himself. Both father and son have been arrested numerous times on meth-related charges and both their lives are centered around the monster. What chance does any son or daughter have when he or she is raised not only using drugs, but using with his or her parents? If it's okay for mom and dad, it must be okay for their child, too. It's what the child knows.

In some cases, as with the teenage boy whose mother forced him to quit school, the child and parent reverse roles. Meth robs individuals of their ability to reason and make practical, mature decisions. One case that brings this point home involved a woman who had been arrested dozens of times for drug-related offenses, including forgery, theft, burglary, and methamphetamine possession. The woman's record spanned two decades and a warrant was finally issued for her arrest. When the woman became aware of the warrant, she found herself in a quandary: should she run to another state or should she turn herself in to the police? She was torn, and so she turned to her ten-year-old daughter for advice. The woman actually told her daughter that whatever her daughter chose—jail or flight—she would do. Can you imagine placing such a monumental decision in the hands of a ten-year-old? I cannot. If the daughter chose jail, she would no doubt always believe that her mom was incarcerated because of her decision. If, on the other hand, the daughter chose flight, she would likely feel responsible that her mom was a fugitive from justice. In the end, the daughter made the mature, responsible choice her mom could not make and advised her mom to turn herself in to the authorities.

Methamphetamine is poison, and the name Ellen Hopkins gave it in *Crank*, "the monster," was very apt. What better name for a drug that deprives children of their right to be a child. Children of meth addicts are most always forced to make adult decisions, and most ultimately end up being users themselves. Children are undoubtedly the biggest victims of the meth epidemic.

I have been told by many experts that meth use promotes sexual promiscuity. Of course, promiscuity involves unprotected sex, which results ultimately in pregnancies. The number of young pregnant mothers who continue to use meth during pregnancy is shocking. I can't begin to count the number of times I have seen pregnant women test positive for meth. I'm not talking about someone who is in the first trimester and doesn't yet know she's pregnant; I'm referring to women who are obviously, noticeably pregnant and still using meth. The effects on their children are devastating. The children are usually born addicted to meth and have many physical and developmental problems. When a girl or woman is pregnant and using meth, the unborn baby—not even yet a part of our world— has already been devastated by meth.

I see many cases of young meth-addicted parents with toddlers. The police or social service workers will go to their homes and find the conditions disgusting, unsanitary, and dangerous. It is common for users to leave hypodermic devices and meth pipes in places that little children have access to, and of course kids are curious and love to explore and touch things they shouldn't. It is also common to find garbage throughout the home and food rotting in dishes that have been sitting out for weeks. Another common discovery is uncared-for animals also living in the squalor, with feces and urine visible on the floors. These conditions aren't fit for the animals let alone the children.

The saddest thing to me is that most all of these young addicted parents love their children, and know that what they are doing is wrong. They know that if they do not free themselves from meth, they will be robbing their children of a childhood and a future. But they continue ruining their children's lives. Most young addicted parents are actually still children themselves.

As a judge, I have seen hundreds of young meth users ruin their lives and the lives of their families, and I have wondered what could be done to stop the carnage. What could I do or say that would make these young people stop using meth? After years of wrestling with these questions, I have finally come to the realization that the judicial system alone cannot fix their problems. Neither can law enforcement, social services, schools, churches, or even families, not alone. Methamphetamine is a monster, and it must be hit from every possible angle. Meth is a community problem and must be addressed by the entire community.

Many people have the misconception that methamphetamine is a problem that affects only those in lower-income, uneducated, dysfunctional families. This is dead wrong. Just in my community alone, I have seen sons and daughters of politicians, law enforcement officers, doctors, lawyers, and high-ranking government officials addicted to meth. I have also seen business people, a religious minister, and athletes fall prey to the monster. In a nearby community, a college president with a doctorate degree succumbed to meth. It is very true that lower-income families have been hit with the scourge of meth, and they have been hit hard. But so has the rest of the community. No sector has been left untouched. And because the problem is community-wide, the solution must be too.

In my community, Carson City, Nevada, a few years ago our mayor and the Board of Supervisors conducted a survey to find out what issues our citizens felt were most important and needed attention. The number one uncontroverted answer was methamphetamine. In response, the mayor, with the support of the Board of Supervisors, the sheriff, and the district attorney, formed a coalition called Partnership Carson City, a steering committee composed of representatives from a broad spectrum of our community. The committee includes the mayor, sheriff, district attorney, superintendent of our schools, chief of probation, and editor of the local newspaper; executive directors of the Community Counseling Center, the Council on Youth, and the Chamber of Commerce; a representative of our local hospital; and myself. Partnership Carson City also formed several sub-committees focused on education, awareness, law enforcement, and counseling.

We developed brochures, posters, and stickers, and created PowerPoint presentations emphasizing how various aspects of our community, including schools, parents, businesses, and government agencies, could help make a difference in the fight against meth. We gave the presentations at schools for parents, at service clubs, in local churches, and to various business groups. Our goal was to inform everyone of the horrible consequences of methamphetamine. We told parents what to look for, the signs a child who is using meth might display. We told the same to school teachers and school counselors. With all the awareness and education, there has been increased need for treatment. It has been amazing to see families come forward and seek help. The Community Counseling Center was prepared, and has accommodated the escalating need for evaluation and counseling.

In the last two years, Carson City has not seen methamphetamine use increase over prior years. In fact, it may have even decreased—not a lot, but at least the growth has stopped. I'm not telling you all this about Partnership Carson City to brag, although I am proud, but instead to convey the message that the entire community must come together to successfully rise above the monster. We haven't stopped meth use but we have definitely made a significant dent.

The bottom line is that awareness and education are critical in stopping illicit drug use. Ellen Hopkins, by providing an insider's view of addiction in *Crank* and *Glass*, is providing another form of education. It was a courageous act for Ellen to share her family's painful struggle with addiction, and by doing so, Ellen has allowed her readers to see and understand the absolute horrors of methamphetamine from a user's perspective—not just from some adult lecturing in a classroom or from a judge's bench. I know that *Crank* and *Glass* have given me insight into addiction that I otherwise would not have. The far-reaching effects of Ellen's books cannot be measured, but I have no doubt she has saved many young people from ever trying this insidious drug.

Judge John Tatro has been Justice of the Peace/Municipal Court Judge in Carson City since 1995. John attended Boise State University and Western Nevada Community College. As a judge, John Tatro has achieved the educational level of Distinguished Jurist. He served as President of the Nevada Judges of Limited Jurisdiction in 2008, and serves on numerous committees and commissions of the Nevada Supreme Court.

In his community, Carson City, Nevada, Judge Tatro serves on Partnership Carson City, an anti-methamphetamine coalition, and the Governor's Working Group on Methamphetamine. He is the Vice-President of Circle of Support, an organization to end homelessness.

John is on the Board of Directors of the Boys & Girls Club of Western Nevada and is a member of the Rotary Club of Carson City.

Judge Tatro lives in Carson City with his wife Kathy, and they have three children, Don, Adrienne, and Nick, as well as one English bulldog, Sherman Tank.

Like a sparrow, captured
in a cage of your own making,
wings braced for flight,
still you fear the opened door.

My child, my child,
I want to hold you harbored
there, secure from claw and talon.
But you beat your feathers

against the bars, cry out
for freedom and I know I must chase
you away, far from my heart,
or witness your slow suicide.

An old proverb says, "If you love something, set it free. If it returns, it's yours forever; if not, it was never meant to be." Sounds reasonable. But what if that "something" is your child, and setting her free (or more accurately, pushing her out the door) might mean she *won't* come back, ever? No parent wants to make that decision, or face having to choose "tough love." But what, argues Gail Giles, if taking yourself out of the picture is the only way to make your child change her destiny? Was excising Kristina from our lives the only way to save her?

Letting a Loved One Go

(Even If You Have to Push)

Gail Giles

"**I** love you, but I can't be around you. I don't want to see you again, ever."

Have you said those words to anyone? Have you wanted to? Is it ever a good thing to cut someone you love out of your life? Can it really be done?

There are myriad themes worthy of discussion in Ellen Hopkins' *Crank* and *Glass*, the story of Kristina's descent into, rehabilitation from, and relapse into crystal meth addiction: addiction itself, the two personalities of Kristina/Bree, the predator/prey relationship of dealer/addict, and the magnitude, scope, and depth of the hurt involved. But the thing that hit me most deeply was the question faced by Kristina's family: When is it enough? When do the people around the addict say, "The wound is too deep. The only thing left is to try and stop the bleeding, to keep the poison for spreading"? Stopping the bleeding means cutting off the blood supply. And that means a tourniquet.

I think that's a good metaphor here. To save Kristina, her family chooses to stop enabling her, to cut her off from their love and support. But is it enough to save her life?

It's not a decision they make lightly. They know it might be what pushes Kristina to her final decline. But that's the time to make it. When the person is going to die anyway. When he or she is bent on self destruction *with* you, there is no other course than to try taking yourself away to change his or her destiny.

In *Crank*, but especially in *Glass*, help and support are actually toxic to Kristina. For reasons not quite understood, they poison her as much as the meth does. My best reading of Kristina is that she always had low self-worth, having been abandoned by her father—it is him as much as Buddy she is trying to please by using meth initially. The guilt of returning to her mother's home an addict, lying, and then getting pregnant intensifies her feeling of being unworthy.

When her family supports her, she is grateful, but when she becomes bored as a single parent, when she resents the work it took, it makes her feel even more guilty, and that guilt disguises itself as anger. The guilt needs to be stamped out. And only meth can do that. "See, I told you I was a loser," Kristina seems to be screaming over and again.

What can her family do? They love her. They want to help. But forgiving her and offering her help is telling her that she cannot do it on her own. That she is a loser. That she will always need them to pick up her load and carry it for her. They must walk away. They must stay away. They must leave Kristina to decide on her own if she is going to be a loser or if she will take hold of her own destiny.

An essential you learn in first aid is that you only apply a tourniquet (no matter what you see on television) if the only option left to save the person's life is the loss of the injured limb. You only apply a tourniquet if you are intending to amputate the limb. And so the metaphor works in another way as well. Cutting someone off, when they have become toxic, is also a way to save yourself. Kristina was poisoning every member of her family, and indeed her friends, each time she dealt with them. The choice to cut Kristina off was necessary not just for Kristina's sake, but for their own.

But what if you are a teen, and the toxic person or persons are your parents or guardians? How do you apply the tourniquet, how do you amputate, then? If you are fourteen years old and your parents physically abuse you—you might be able to turn to child protection services for help. Depending on the proof, and the depth and breadth of the abuse, you might be removed from the home. And then you take your chances with the system. I have to be honest here. How bad is the abuse? If it is sexual, make the call. Get out now. If the physical abuse has sent you to the hospital, make the call. Otherwise, find an adult, a counselor, a teacher—someone you trust—to talk to. Let them guide you.

What I faced was emotional and mild physical abuse. A lot of it was accepted socially at that time, but it was still painful and confusing. Damaging. I thought it was normal for years. When I realized that other people didn't treat their children this way, I was faced with a dilemma. Did I accept this and buckle under, did I rage against it and become an angry, disruptive, abusive person who resembled my parents? I found another way. And in teaching high school, I've come across other teens who have found that same survivor's path. Yes, we apply the tourniquet. We cut our parents off. In most cases, we do it by understanding that they are wrong. We are not stupid, losers, always wrong, and not—I repeat, *not*—worthless. We tie that artery off and let it wither and die. Yes, some of our ability to love and respect die with it. But in that artery's place an awareness blooms. We are young. Not finished. We do need guidance and nurturing. We are not ready to go it alone. We cannot. And so we search. I looked, and the students I've met looked, to the parents of our friends. Whose parents showed us the nurturing we were looking for? Which could provide what our own parents did not? I was lucky to find someone close at hand. My best friend's mother was not only kind, she was smart and she was no nonsense. She set boundaries and expected you to operate within them. I both wanted and needed that. But the wonderful thing was, the boundaries were always the same. They didn't change according to the frustrations and moods of their maker. When I did something wrong I knew why. I learned to take responsibility for my actions, because the response I received because of them wasn't arbitrary.

While you have to cut off a limb, you learn to grab onto a shoulder for support. Just make sure the shoulder is the right support.

So what if you don't cut off that person—if the limb is not amputated? If you continue your relationship with the toxic person? Gangrene. Gangrene may start in a lower limb, but quickly spreads and kills the rest of the organism, and that's also true in a relationship and the people in it.

What would have happened had Kristina's family not completely cut her off? Remaining in their life, she would have poisoned every one of them. Her mother's marriage would have been ruined, her child would have ended up dysfunctional, her mother and older sister's relationship would have been irreparable. Too many people's lives were at stake *not* to make the choice they did.

And Kristina? If her family had not cut her off, she would never have recovered. She uses them like she uses the drug; when using glass gets too hard, she retreats to the drug of her parents help to pick up the pieces. When she overdoses on her family's support, she just returns to glass and the behavior necessary to procure it. Amputation is a way to stop that cycle. Maybe the only one.

That isn't to say that the choice isn't hard. Amputation is losing a part of yourself, and cutting yourself off from someone you love is not much different. But this leaves us with one last question: *Can you cut a person out of your life?* If you are an adult, then physically, yes. You can walk away, you can choose to not turn back. You cannot talk to, see, or touch them again. Can you stop loving and caring for them? I guess it depends on the amount and nature of the damage they have done, but I think if you get down to hard reality—no. Amputation of a limb is said to produce "phantom limb syndrome." The amputee still feels the missing limb—feels pain in it, feels it itch, feels the weight of it. How can it not be the same with a loved one we cut out of our life? We may not see or speak to them. But they are our "phantom limb"—we remember shared experiences, we feel their presence, we want to turn and tell them something. They are in our dreams and our memories. They are still part of us. I think the best we can do is hope that the amputation was successful, and fill the hole the phantom limb leaves behind with love and hope.

It is said that you cannot remember pain. But I think, or possibly I hope, that you do remember what made you love someone in the first place, what made you hope. That always stays with you. Emily Dickinson was so correct: "Hope is the thing with feathers." And it always struggles to fly.

Gail Giles was born during a hurricane on Galveston Island many years ago. She refuses to give the exact year, but does assure us that it was not the 1900 storm. She keeps running from hurricanes by moving as often as she can, from Texas to Chicago to Indiana to Alaska and back to Texas, where the storms keep finding her. Her books are dark, psychological thrillers but she swears she has yet to murder anyone except in fiction. She has three dogs, one husband, one son, and two grandsons.

Look
        through tear-streaked windows
        to harbors, wide and still.
        And floating there like
driftwood,
        unanchored in the silence,
        confessions left unspoken. Muted
        by the deep, a current of
deception
        coaxes them toward the rocks.

Listen
        as the tide begins to swell,
        spitting out the sorrow,
        concealed within its
secrets.
        Do you hear it mourning
        for innocence waning, and love left
        fading within the shadow of lies?

Secrets. Seems to me, pretty much everybody has at least one or two they're trying to keep from someone else. Then there are the secrets other people ask you to keep for them, whether or not you should. Is it healthy to keep secrets? Does keeping them basically mean you're lying to someone else—or yourself? Terri Clark answers these questions, and poses another: With so many of my characters invested in their personal deceptions, what is it with me and secrets anyway?

The Secret's Out

Terri Clark

We who have a voice must speak for the voiceless.
—ARCHBISHOP OSCAR ROMERO

Ellen Hopkins has a voice, one that speaks in rhythm and verse, with truth and grit. She speaks for the voiceless, revealing their tragedies, exposing their complex personal layers, whispering their secrets. In lyrical tones and sparse but striking words she delves into the darkness many real-life teens find themselves in. She tells the stories they hide from or hold tight to their chests.

The endings of those stories aren't always happy, but then again neither is reality. Because of this Ellen refuses to tie things up with a perfect, pretty bow. When a reader fussed about her endings on a message board, Ellen responded by saying, "Life rarely ties everything up nicely, and while often novels do, those feel-good endings are contrived. I'd rather give you honesty."

And that she does.

Her books tackle tough, often taboo, topics like addiction; rape; physical, emotional and sexual abuse; suicide; cutting; alcoholism; repression; neglect; mental illness; incest; and prostitution. While few would dare, Ellen Hopkins steps into the shadows and embraces the secrets stashed there. She shatters the silence.

Ask her if she realizes what a strong theme secrets are in her work and she says, "Of course. In all my books. Secrets kept. Secrets exposed. Secrets confessed, but no one will listen. But almost every piece of good literature has a secret in it somewhere."

So what is it with Ellen and secrets?

What is it with teens and secrets?

For Ellen, at least, the story begins with her own daughter's secrets. As everyone is by now aware, *Crank* is loosely based on Ellen's daughter's meth addiction. *Glass*, its sequel, is even more biographical. Ellen has stated that she wrote *Crank* from her daughter's perspective so she could better understand "Kristina" and better understand her own part in her child's downward spiral. The result is a raw, painful, poignant, and intense study of secrets and their destructive power.

The Secret's Out

Was Ellen ever afraid of revealing the problems her family had kept private?

> I *started Crank* out of anger, frustration, the need to understand. So basically I just started writing. It became evident fairly quickly, however, that my family would be exposed some, which is why I chose to fictionalize as heavily as I did. For instance, I created an older daughter and younger son. In real life, I have an older son and younger daughter. Some of the characters are also composites of real people, to give the real-life players a small sense of anonymity. As I've moved forward, however, I've found it more important to share the stories honestly. So now, I have little fear of secrets being exposed because I've basically "confessed" most everything.

For Ellen, stripping away the secrets didn't make her vulnerable, it empowered her because it left nothing there for her to fear.

It's that realization that each of her characters must come to in their own way.

There's a scene in *Crank* where Kristina's family tries, over lasagna and garlic bread, to coax details out of her about that summer at her father's. She tells a sanitized version of the truth, but omits the most profound event that happened to her . . . her introduction to "the monster." However, it's quickly apparent her sister, Leigh, senses something more:

Leigh knew
there was a
whole lot

             more

to the story,
of course.
But I'd never
told her

             secrets,

and trusted
completely
she would
never betray

             mine.

Still, just in
case, I
never dared
mention

             sex,

interrupted
by periods;
Lince,
interrupted by

             drugs;

or my own
infatuation with

the monster's
spectacular

                rock and roll.

No, these
secrets
belonged strictly
in my own
private closet. [*emphasis mine*]

What would've happened if she'd told Leigh or her mom? Perhaps Kristina would've gotten help sooner and never been raped by Brendan, become a drug dealer for the Mexican Mafia, and gotten pregnant with a baby she was ill-prepared to take care of. Of course, hindsight is 20/20 and you can never know where the path you're on might veer, but what if? Isn't it that question that ultimately drives secrets?

What if?

What if I tell?

What if I don't?

When Kristina finally tells her parents, after nearly terminating her pregnancy, her mom and step-dad go through an understandable tornado of emotions before promising to be there for her and the baby as long as she finishes school. But what if she'd never told them? What if they'd reacted differently? What if she'd actually gone through with the abortion?

What if?

It's the fear of the unknown, the inability to predict the future, and often our lack of faith in ourselves or others that presses us into keeping secrets.

Sometimes, the biggest secrets we keep are from ourselves. In *Impulse*, Tony, Vanessa, and Connor are locked up in the Aspen Springs psych hospital because of the secrets they keep. Tony was sexually molested by his mother's boyfriend when he was eight. Later, he prostituted himself for drugs, and now he's questioning his sexuality. Vanessa had an abortion no one knows about, struggles with bi-polarism, and cuts herself to relieve her mental anguish. To the outside world, Connor looks like a flawless, privileged boy, but his cold, uncaring parents' constant pressure for perfection has driven him into a depression. He also has an unhealthy preoccupation with older women, and when a repressed memory finally comes into focus, he realizes that desire stems from a twisted need for physical love.

Three teens.

A surfeit of secrets.

When the secrets come out—in therapy, among friends, amidst self discovery—what happens? Two of them find healing. And although the road ahead is hard and filled with uncertainty, they feel better equipped to deal with the pressure and changes. For Vanessa, cutting is actually a physical manifestation, a symbolic release, of her hidden demons. The secrets she bottled up cause her great pain, but fear keeps her from letting them go. So she spills them with blood, tries to release their poison with a different kind of pain. Maybe, too, she bleeds so someone would take a closer look and peer beyond her camouflage.

I cut to focus when my

brain is racing.

I cut to make physical

what I feel inside.

I cut to see blood

because I like it.

I don't like to cut,

but I can't give it up.

Fortunately, the more she emotionally reveals herself throughout the book, the deeper she falls in love with Tony, the less she feels driven to mutilate herself. Having found help, having found love, Tony and Vanessa are able to surpass their secrets and come out stronger in the end. For Connor, it's not such a happy ending—but then, he gives up, gives in, quits fighting. He continues keeping secrets and they lead him off a ledge.

One thing Ellen's books demonstrate is that strength of spirit is necessary to tame our hidden truths. Her characters, ordinary as they may be, are extraordinary because of the courage they exhibit in facing their demons. There's an old quote that says, "Anyone can give up, it's the easiest thing in the world to do. But to hold it together when everyone else would understand if you fell apart, that's true strength." Ellen Hopkins understands the fortitude that's necessary to be that courageous.

She also grasps, wrenching as it is, that some teens, like Connor, don't feel powerful enough to fight the darkness. In *Burned*, Pattyn Von Stratten is a good Mormon girl who begins to question her

religion, her place in life, and her physically abusive father. Her defi-
ance gets her sent to her aunt's where she discovers a whole different
world, an inner strength she never knew she possessed, and a forever
kind of love. Her romance turns tragic when Patty learns she's pregnant. Ultimately, she loses her family, her baby, and her boyfriend.
Distraught and alone Patty waffles between committing suicide or
taking revenge, with a 10mm gun, on the people who ruined her
life. The reader is left wondering what happened next.

Did she crack and go Columbine on her fellow church members,
her classmates, her dad? Or did she peer over the freeway overpass
she sat on and simply let herself slide off the railing, ending it all?
Maybe, God willing, she found a third choice, a moment of clarity
amidst her madness. Perhaps she didn't follow through with either
plan and instead walked away to loudly scream the secrets she'd
long been hiding. Maybe, as she bobbed between two bad choices,
her memories would stir. . . .

Ethan, her love, once told her, "Pattyn, we are nothing if we can't
tell each other our secrets."

Freedom.

Shortly thereafter, following her father's bludgeoning blows, her
dad said, "Family secrets stay behind these doors."

Prison.

Secrets shackled the Von Strattens and only Ellen Hopkins
knows what happened next. She says she's toying with the idea for a
sequel, but one thing is certain: secrets are destructive.

Had Patty exposed her bruises and unmasked her father, would
she have been able to save her sister, herself, their futures? Going

one step further, if her aunt had revealed her brother's volatility and malignance after being threatened at gunpoint, instead of running away, could she have spared her nieces? Are secrets a legacy to be passed down from generation to generation?

The answer should be no. But is there ever a time when a secret protects a person more than it harms them? Presented with that question, Ellen says, "I think there are times when keeping mum about something like an affair is perhaps the best choice. As long as NO ONE ELSE KNOWS. And there's the rub. Because if someone else knows the secret, it's bound to get out sooner or later. People love 'telling,' don't they?"

That they do, and isn't it better to be the one who tells the tale, in your own way, in your own time, rather than having the proverbial rug yanked out from underneath you when someone else tattles? Besides, what's the likelihood a secret is ever truly yours and yours alone?

And even if it is, what does that do to you? Does the secret eat away at your insides like a metastasizing cancer? Does it distress you to present one face to everyone else and see another reflected in the mirror? Do you come to realize that keeping mum is really speaking lies?

Secrets equal lies. Whether it's an act of omission or an outright lie to divert attention from what's being concealed, read Ellen's work and you'll see that secrets equate to falsehoods and those untruths often build upon themselves until the perjurer is thoroughly entangled in a sticky web of their own making.

For Kristina, lies pile upon lies. Each seduction by the monster bolsters her need to fib so the drug won't be stripped from her:

Flirtin' with the Monster

Kristina, what's going on with you?
I couldn't tell her the truth.
What kind of lies might do? I started
with a genuine, 'I'm sorry.'
Oh, God, I'm sorry too.
She sat down beside me
on the bed, put her arms around
me, hugged tight.
You're not in any trouble, are you?
Trouble? All sorts of trouble, oh,
yes. But not the kind she was worried
about. 'No mom.'

Each fabrication feeds into another as she morphs from a quiet, naïve, inexperienced girl to a hardened, abused and abusive parasite that leeches off anyone who can give her what she wants. She goes from being Kristina to Bree. The question is . . . is Bree her biggest lie or biggest truth?

While Ellen has obviously pondered whether there's ever a good reason to keep a secret, her work seems to imply the answer is no.

Secrets.
We keep them to protect ourselves.
We keep them to protect others.
We keep them out of shame.
We keep them out of fear.
We keep them . . . wait . . . *do we keep them or do they keep us?*

Martin Luther King said, "The day we see the truth and cease to speak is the day we begin to die."

Secrets suffocate. Nowhere is that more apparent than in Ellen's stories. And yet, in writing about secrets, in telling her own deepest, darkest secrets, the most wondrous thing has happened: Secrets have been shared. Many with Ellen.

> This is a daily thing. Sometimes several in a day. I feel a heavy responsibility because many of these secrets should be shared, and I am charged with keeping them. I will say if I feel someone is in danger, I do everything in my power to get him or her to tell someone who can help in a more tangible way than just being an ear. I have been relatively successful at that, and know I've helped more than a few people find help for depression, cutting, drug use and abuse.

The feminist writer Robin Morgan once said, "Silence is the first thing within the power of the enslaved to shatter. From that shattering, everything else spills forth."

Are you ready to shatter the silence?

Share your secret?

Speak.

There are people willing to listen. . . .

Terri Clark feels blessed to demonstrate her passion for young adult fiction as both a teen librarian and young adult author. Terri writes paranormal fiction and had the pleasure of participating in the anthology, *Breaking Up Is Hard To Do*, with Ellen Hopkins. Her debut book, *Sleepless*, came out shortly thereafter and is about a teen psychic who is pursued in her sleep by a killer. Terri lives in Colorado with her husband, two children, and their adorkable dog, Domino. You can visit her online at www.terriclarkbooks.com.

Id confronts ego.
Kristina succumbs to Bree.
It's enough to make poor
Sigmund somersault in his grave.
All or nothing at all generally
leads to the latter.

Middle ground may feel
tenuous, riddled with faults.
Earthquake territory. But monsters
of varied temperaments
patrol its potholed borders.

Good. Bad. Something in between. Every human being carries some combination of these inside. Ego is our conscious awareness, the part of us that tells us what we should do. Id is our instinct, and as we're animals after all, should the id get the upper hand, trouble often follows. Bree is the id to Kristina's ego, and eventually Bree gets the upper hand. But does Kristina, in fact, allow that to happen? Micol Ostow says yes, and wonders why she couldn't instead find middle ground.

The Importance of Being Between

Micol Ostow

In-Between Places

If you've ever had any occasion to visit my official author website, you might know that it describes me as "half Puerto Rican, half Jewish, half student, half writer, half chocolate, half peanut butter." I'm here to tell you that it's all true, every last word. I am a mutt, through and through. And darn proud of it.

Full disclosure, though: I haven't always been as comfortable with my mixed-breed status as I am these days. Anyone grappling with a diverse ethnic or cultural background (which, I would venture to say, is most of us) knows from the experience of constantly wanting to check the "other" box on the questionnaire of Life, probably all too well. As if it were that simple, defining ourselves by the things we are not (in my case: patient, blonde, and mathematically inclined, just for starters). As if the very act of labeling ourselves—carefully, definitively, unwaveringly—were what cements our sense of both collective and individual identity.

I'm not buying it.

Not only am I determined to argue that we need to embrace all facets of ourselves, as a whole, but I'd offer that in fact, to do otherwise—to rigidly compartmentalize our less appealing personality traits—is the stuff of madness-making. Or, put another way: if we ignore little pieces of our own respective personalities, we can (and do) literally drive ourselves crazy.

In other words, each of our beings—mind, body, spirit—is made from the *sum* of its parts (another little piece of questionable website wisdom, and the reason why I'm so into Chubby Hubby ice cream: lots of gooey, delicious parts all mushed up together). *We*, in essence, are made up of the stuff that generally slips through the cracks: the in-between. And to deny our own "between-ness" is what I like to think of as general Bad Idea-itis. It can lead to confusion, anxiety, and maybe, in certain worst-case scenarios, some fairly self-destructive choices.

I suspect that "Kristina Snow" would agree with me.

Good Cop/Bad Cop

As high school students, Kristina and I actually had a few things in common, once upon a time. At first glance, Kristina seems as pure and driven as her name would suggest: "straight-A," "talented," the "perfect daughter," and a "gifted student." She acknowledges that her life, her *self*, may even be "enviable."

Of course, like most of us, Kristina has a dirty little secret: an alter-ego to whom she is all too eager to introduce us. Enter Bree.

Bree is the foil to Kristina's heroine. Bree is "not quite silent," "not quite sanitary," and, frankly, Kristina herself admits, "not quite sane." At first, Bree emerges only when Kristina is alone, "a distorted reality" but still, in some ways, exactly what Kristina needs. Kristina claims to like Bree better than she likes her stuffy, stuck-up, solemn (but true) self, which often feels like an empty "husk." Bree is who Kristina conjures when "dreams no longer satisfy, when gentle clouds of monotony smother thunder."

"When Kristina cries." I think we can all relate.

The Part with the Science

But let's back up for a moment, shall we? Let's get a little bit fancy. Let's talk Sigmund Freud, the big old grandfather of psychology.

He was pretty smart, old Siggy, and he had this idea that our mind (that is to say, the function of it, not the actual organ, the brain) is driven by three basic forces that interact together to govern our internal choices and external actions: the super-ego, the id, and the ego.

The id is the dark, inaccessible side of our personality. It's our unconscious desires: our dirty little secrets. Conveniently, the id can be defined in a flurry of "i-words": impulse, instinct, internal. It's everything we wish, but would probably be loathe to say out loud. The id demands immediate satisfaction; the id will not be denied. Sound like anyone you know? Anyone you've read about, maybe?

(I'll give you a hint: it rhymes with "tree.")

Yeah, the id's a lot like Bree. For better or for worse.

The super-ego is the opposite of the id. Contrary to what its label may suggest, the super-ego is not a caped crusader of the mind. It is, however, meant to fight against the forces of evil, or at least the forces of pure, unbridled pleasure-seeking—in other words, the id.

Generally speaking, the super-ego is not a whole lot of fun. It's the part of your mind that makes you feel guilty for blowing off studying, exercising, or saving your money. In laymen's terms, it's your conscience. Technically, the super-ego's job is to remind you of all the things society and your parents tell you that you should be doing. A whole lot of the time, what it feels like it's doing is raining on your personal parade. The super-ego can be a real buzz-kill.

Which brings us to the ego. If the ego were a superhero, it might be called the Compromiser. It's forever trying to find a compromise between the wanting of the id and the rules and restrictions of the super-ego, and it's what helps us go about our day-to-day lives as generally reasonable human beings. The ego is the little voice that tells us to study if we want to pass the test, to exercise if we want to be healthy, to get a job and save our money toward something that we really, really want. In Latin, "ego" actually translates to "I, myself." These days we tend to use the word "ego" colloquially to mean our self-esteem, especially in the case of *excessive* ego, or arrogance, but that's a bit of a leap from how the term translates clinically.

Most of us, most of the time, are able to manage the delicate push-and-pull balance between the super-ego and the id. Our egos keep us in check. While there are days when we eat all of our vegetables, study hard, and hit the sack early, we also have days when we stuff ourselves on pizza and ice cream and OD on reality TV. (Feel free to insert your own comparable metaphor for responsibility/hedonism here.) In other words, most of us are usually able to navigate the in-between.

But what happens when we can't? When things become too all-or-nothing, one-or-the-other, right-or-wrong? Well, why don't we ask Kristina?

In Her Own Words

When Kristina describes Bree, it's as a wholly unique, individual separate from her "real," self. Bree first emerges when Kristina pays a summer visit to her long-lost deadbeat father.

It's an anticlimactic reunion. While Kristina's mother has warned her of her father's various and innumerable less-than-appealing habits, she's still not fully prepared for the wordless chasm that exists between them when they feebly attempt conversation, for her father's substandard living arrangements, for the fact that he hasn't told his current girlfriend that he even has a daughter.

The situation is not ideal, to say the least.

Shortly after her arrival, Kristina encounters a sexy, mysterious stranger. He's a neighbor, and he seems as intrigued by her as she is with him, which bland, upstanding "Kristina" can't quite fathom. When it's time for formal introductions, she hesitates only for a moment: "My friends call me Bree."

It's not a lie, not *exactly*. But *which* friends? Not Kristina's usual school crowd, that's for sure. Bree is carefully hidden from that crew.

The stranger introduces himself as Adam. (Though it's worth noting that he, too, has a nickname of his own: Buddy. Hopkins is fully committed to exploring dualities in her work.) Kristina begins a new life during those three weeks, one which is principally defined by the presence—the *dominance*—of Bree.

"What was up with this person, Bree?" Kristina asks herself. "And was she a permanent fixture?" By distancing herself from Bree, Kristina is able to divorce herself completely from the increasingly unhealthy decisions that her shadow-self pursues. On the subject of choices, she says, "It seems to Kristina you gotta be crazy to open your windows, invite the demons in. Bree throws rocks at the feeble glass, laughs."

And Bree definitely doesn't know what's good for Kristina, or for herself, to be honest. She leaps into a sexual relationship with Adam despite knowing that he's already involved with someone else, and shortly thereafter, she makes her first attempt at flirting with the monster, or crystal meth. She can't believe herself, her behavior, doesn't know where any of it comes from.

If it's a cry for help, it doesn't work. When Kristina's father finds her high, in a bathroom, with Adam, he joins them for a line. The situation quickly spirals (even further) out of control.

Kristina may expect that a return to her hometown of Reno and her "real life" will mean a return to her former self, but it's not to be. Bree, Kristina's id, has run rampant by this point, and sees no escape from the monster. Bree is hooked.

Which means that Kristina is, too.

The Doppleganger Effect, or: More Science, Sort of

With the invention of Bree, Kristina may be playing at Dr. Jekyll and Mr. Hyde, but the reality is that true multiple personality disorder is actually somewhat rare out there in the real world. The clinical term for the condition is *Dissociative Identity Disorder*, and it's characterized by the display of multiple personalities, each with its own pattern of perceiving and interacting with the environment. In order to be diagnosed with the disorder, one must be controlled by at least two separate personalities, each with little to no memory of the other or others.

And here's the thing: personality shifts and/or memory loss driven by substance abuse don't count.

DID is considered a controversial diagnosis. In fact, some doctors think it's unique to North America. But one thing most researches can agree on is that people who display the symptoms of this disorder have often suffered from sexual abuse. And yes, as Kristina allows Bree out to play, she finds herself growing increasingly precocious, increasingly promiscuous. She has her first kiss as Bree, and later, loses her virginity as Bree to a date-rapist. These are certainly the sort of experiences that would encourage one to seek escape, perhaps in the form of an alternate persona. But that doesn't mean that Bree is actually a different persona than Kristina—as much as Kristina might want her to be.

By allowing Bree to make the hard decisions (and often the ill-advised ones, too), Kristina divorces herself from the responsibility of living her own life. Not only does she create a new personality for herself whole cloth, she even personifies the drug which has her in its grip. Few would argue with the idea that addiction can take over an individual to the exclusion of their free will, but meth itself is not a sentient being with actual motives or drive. Meth is, at least in the early stages of their "relationship," a choice that Kristina makes. Or, if not Kristina, then Bree.

But really—what's the difference?

As it turns out, not that much at all.

I Know You Are, But What Am I?

The truth of the matter is, even Kristina herself admits (however reluctantly) that, when all is said and done, Bree is *not*, in fact, a separate entity, but rather an extension of herself. What's more, Kristina is well aware that Bree has always been there, deep inside. "Spare me those Psych '01 labels," she says, "I'm no more schizo than most. Bree is no imaginary playmate, no overactive pituitary, no alter ego, moving in. Hers is the face I wear, treading the riptide, fathomless oceans where good girls drown."

"Besides," she argues, "even good girls have secrets, ones even their best friends must guess."

But no one *does* guess. Or in any event, those who do are pushed away (Kristina withdraws from her "good girl" friends early on in the story). Once she's met the monster, Bree has no further need for good girls.

Still, Kristina speaks of "our," and "we," suggesting a base level awareness of her own in-between state, even as she seeks to divide herself from the basest drives of her id. Bree comes and goes at Kristina's will, because at the core, Bree and Kristina are one. Had Kristina managed to find a balance, to find the in-between of her "true" self and her Bree self, the place where the two intersect to create a more whole being, she may not have ultimately needed the monster to help her escape her own black-and-white paradigms. The monster is Kristina's mechanism for obliterating her secret drives—for placing them outside and away from herself—and Bree is Kristina's mechanism for choosing the monster without actually having to confront that choice.

Hard decisions sometimes become easier when we've convinced ourselves that they are out of our hands. And so it is for Kristina. Addiction is a fierce, painful grip, monstrous indeed. But despite the conflicting forces of peer and family pressure, school, and the other stresses that face today's teen, the choice to shake hands with the monster—*any* monster—is always, in the end, entirely our own.

I can't pretend to have lived Bree's story, or even Kristina's. But I do know what it's like to constantly feel as though you're coming up short. I'm not religious enough, I'm not Latina enough, I'm always either/or. But I refused to define myself—or to allow myself to be defined—as "other."

Honestly? Half-and-half is really, truly, not half bad.

I genuinely believe that if we as individuals can acknowledge (and maybe even appreciate) our own cracks, our personal contradictions, and our in-between spaces, we might find ourselves with less need to escape, or to fully deny any side of ourselves. Kristina, Bree, Jewish, Puerto Rican, chocolate, peanut butter—we can be all things to ourselves (and maybe even—eventually—to others, as well), and make healthy, active decisions. *If* we embrace the whole, rather than just the parts.

Crank and *Glass* are poignant, evocative, lyrical, and thought-provoking stories, to be sure. Kristina/Bree's tandem journey is a heartbreaking cautionary tale. And while Kristina/Bree's story does not end as hopefully as I, as a reader, would like it to, my own hope for her/them is that they are able to finally, ultimately, come together. And possibly find some middle ground.

Micol Ostow has written more than forty published works for children, tweens, and teens, including *Emily Goldberg Learns to Salsa*, a New York Public Library Book for the Teen Age. Micol's hybrid graphic novel project, *So Punk Rock (and Other Ways to Disappoint Your Mother)*, will release in July 2009, and will feature rockin' (literally) illustrations from her younger brother, David Ostow. In the mean-time, she is hard at work on The Bradford Novels, a scandalicious new series about privileged Philadelphia private school girls and featuring extensive online content. Micol has an MFA in Writing for Children and Young Adults from Vermont College of the Fine Arts, and teaches young adult writing up and down the East Coast. Visit her at: www.micolostow.com.

Truth is little more than
a five-letter word, inconclusive,
constrained by perception.

Filter any single incident
through another pair of eyes,
it becomes a different story.

Striving to write the truth,
the whole truth, and nothing but,
compels the writer to lie.

I chose to write *Crank* and *Glass* as fiction, loosely based on fact. Often, for readers, the line between truth and storytelling becomes blurred, as I wanted it to be. Many have wondered how much of the books really happened, and some have asked why not write the story as memoir instead. Cinda Williams Chima compares memoir as truth versus fiction as truth, and gives her valuable insight into the question, *Can fiction, in fact, speak truer than memoir?*

Reality-Based Memoir vs. Non-Fiction

Cinda Williams Chima

Ellen Hopkins' bestselling verse novels, *Crank* and *Glass*, are based on her real-life experience with her daughter's teenage methamphetamine addiction. In her author's note in *Crank*, she says, "While this work is fiction, it is loosely based on a very true story—my daughter's."

Certainly, Hopkins' direct experience with the consequences of crack addiction inform and lend authenticity to her fiction. Hopkins wrote non-fiction before she became a novelist, so clearly, she has the skills to succeed in that world. Yet she chose to tell her true story in novel form. Why would she do that?

The first problem memoirists encounter these days is convincing skeptical readers that they are telling the truth, thanks to several high-profile memoir scandals that have scalded an already-cynical public.

The most famous example of memoir gone wrong is James Frey's *A Million Little Pieces*, a gritty, supposedly true story of crime, addiction, and redemption. It sold millions of copies after it was chosen for Oprah's Book Club and Frey appeared on *Oprah*.

Shortly after, *The Smoking Gun* website exposed Frey as an unsuccessful novelist who parleyed his history of drug addiction and minor arrest into a sensational memoir larded with exaggerations and made-up events. In real life, an intoxicated Frey drives over a curb. In *AMLP*, he drives over a police officer. That distinction proved to be important to many readers.

Frey isn't the only offender. In her book *Misha: A Memoire of the Holocaust Years*, Belgian author Misha Defonseca claimed that as a little Jewish girl she trekked across Europe, looking for her parents and taking shelter with friendly wolf packs. Her book was a bestseller in Europe, and was eventually made into a movie.

It was later revealed that Defonseca was actually Catholic, and spent the Holocaust years living safely in Brussels.

The most recent example is Margaret Seltzer, a young white woman from well-to-do Sherman Oaks, California, the product of a private day school. She wrote a "memoir," *Love and Consequences*, under the name of Margaret B. Jones. In it, she claimed to have come up as a biracial foster child in South Central Los Angeles, serving as a drug-runner for the Bloods gang. The deception was revealed when her sister saw Seltzer's photo in the *New York Times* book review and contacted her publisher.

The books were subsequently pulped and her author tour cancelled.

Why do memoirists reinvent the truth?

In an interview with the *New York Times*, Seltzer argued that she saw the book as an opportunity to give voice to those that otherwise wouldn't be listened to. "I just felt that there was good that I could do and there was no other way that someone would listen to it."

In a statement confessing that her story was a fabrication, Defonseca defends herself by saying, "This story is mine. It is not actually reality, but my reality, my way of surviving. I ask forgiveness to all who felt betrayed."

Frey says that his book is "emotionally true."

Hopkins has some advice for Frey and the others: call it what it is. "Mr. Frey should have called [AMLP] a novel, loosely based on a real-life experience."

Only Frey tried that before he sold his book as a memoir. When he shopped the work as fiction, publishers turned him down. We are a nation fixated on reality TV and tell-all books. Take fiction and call it a memoir, and it's easier to sell.

Books like Frey's and Defonseca's are viewed as scandalous because they violate the contract between the memoirist and the reader by not meeting readers' expectations of what memoir is.

I would argue that the purpose of memoir is 1) to tell the truth, 2) to deliver story effectively, and 3) to help both the memoirist and the reader make sense of past events.

Memoir is compelling because it is supposedly true. But what is truth? Reviewers, editors, writers, and representatives of the media have varying tolerances for the creative part of creative non-fiction. Confronted with establishing a boundary between memoir and fiction, some react by saying, basically, what's all the fuss about?

This question stuns strict constructionists, many of them trained as journalists. To them, truth is verifiable fact. It's written down in a record somewhere, or collectable through interviews.

In an article in the *New York Times Book Review*, columnist and novelist Anna Quindlen admits that she cannot remember the details that would bring her true stories to life. In the absence of that, she refuses to make them up.

Before she could comfortably say in an essay, "It was very cold the night my mother died," Quindlen had to go back and look up the actual weather records for the day in question to make sure her recollection was truthful. It wasn't enough to be true to her memory.

"I will never write a memoir," says Quindlen, "even though the form has become the *oeuvre du jour*. I've got a lousy memory."

Similarly, former *Washington Post* staffer and now journalism professor Walt Harrington advocates what he calls "reported memoir," a hybrid of journalism, memoir, and essay that is different from what he calls "arm-chair memoir." Presumably, if the "arm-chair" memoirist is missing a fact, she cannot be bothered to research it. She just makes it up.

Reality-Based Memoir vs. Non-Fiction

In an interview with *Poynter Online*, Harrington describes the methods he used to collect data and facts for his hunting memoir, *The Everlasting Stream*.

He approached it like a documentary film-maker. Once he'd decided to write the book, he began carrying a voice-activated recorder in his pocket on his hunting trips. He recorded conversations with the other hunters, along with verbal notes on the weather, animal life, and his own thoughts. He also took numerous photographs.

Harrington later returned to the fields they hunted with a naturalist so that he could report accurately on the plants that grew there, engaged an astronomer to interpret the sky on their hunting mornings, and attended a necropsy on a rabbit at the University of Illinois vet lab so he could detail the process of skinning and gutting a rabbit.

I would say that's extreme. The word *memoir* implies that it is written from memory. Writers must be more attentive than other people, but I have to wonder whether such a self-conscious method creates a true record of "real life" as lived off camera, so to speak. Harrington's colleagues might forget the recorder was there, but he couldn't possibly. Also, when writing, Harrington still picks and chooses, omits and includes, and that shapes the final story.

Does the average reader care whether the memoirist verifies his exact elevation on a soil conservation map? Does it make the book better, more effective? I've not read Harrington's book, but I suspect that what makes it compelling is the "soft parts"—the essay parts, the reflective parts, the parts where Harrington does Job #3, helping the memoirist and the reader make sense of past events. I get the impression that, as a literary writer who labored long in a journalistic world, Harrington is trying too hard to be legit.

There is a more liberal view that holds that the truth can be both more and less than the facts.

Freelance journalist Lindsay Beyerstein gives memoir more wiggle room than other types of non-fiction, although she says that there is a line that should not be crossed. "I'm prepared to accept the memoir/autobiography distinction. However, the 'memoir' label doesn't excuse massive fraud, *a la* James Frey. Memoirs are still a form of non-fiction. Readers are looking to the memoirist for truthiness, if not for literal truth."[1]

Truthiness? Is literal truth so impossible to achieve? Maybe so.

In the *New Yorker*, Jill Lepore points out in reference to the memoir-fiction debate, that we should remember that even what we call "history" is not as factual as we like to think.

This was eloquently demonstrated in James Loewen's book *Lies My Teacher Told Me*. Loewen critiqued twelve commonly used high school history textbooks that distort the true story of history by selecting, shaping, and slanting the facts.

Leowen describes what he calls the process of "heroification," what he calls "a degenerative process, much like calcification, that makes people over into heroes." Leowen argues that the educational media turn real, flawed individuals into "pious, perfect creatures without conflicts, pain, credibility, or human interest."

---

[1] From her blog: http://majikthise.typepad.com/majikthise_/2006/03/memoir_autobiog.html

(You could argue that Frey did the opposite: the anti-heroification of himself.)

Lepore says, "Every history is incomplete; every historian has a point of view; every historian relies on what is unreliable—documents written by people who are not under oath and cannot be cross-examined."

Interestingly, Lepore argues that fiction is more likely to tell truths about women and ordinary people than any "factual" history.

Frey, Seltzer, *et al*, are extreme examples, and do not represent memoir overall. Unfortunately, they have raised questions about the entire genre. They have sacrificed Job #1 (telling the truth) to achieve Job #2 (delivering story). It's hard to imagine they've achieved Job #3—the self-reflection and soulwork that memoir can accomplish. If you know darn well you're lying, writing memoir is unlikely to help you come to terms with your past.

But what about the memoirist who mounts his memoir on the bones of truth, who relays events as best he can remember, but recreates conversations from childhood that he couldn't possibly recall word for word? Or the memoirist that admits in his preface that he combined certain events, changed names, and that "some episodes are not intended to portray actual events."

Why is writing good memoir so difficult to do without fictionalizing?

Many memoirists believe that fictionalizing makes a memoir more readable. In her essay "Memoir? Fiction? Where's the line?" Memoirist Mimi Schwartz says, "If we stick only to facts, our past is as skeletal as black-and-white line drawings in a coloring book.

We must color it in." According to Schwartz, it's the emotional truth that's important.

Writer Linda Joy Myers believes that memoir must mimic fiction in order to engage the reading public. On her blog "Transform Your Life Through Memoir Writing," Meyers says, "[A] memoir writer must create a story that has a shape, drama, and story arc." This might mean changing timelines or adding details to make scenes more vivid. Still, says Myers, "our job is to be as accurate and as honest as we can be."

Others suggest that memoir is, by its very nature, flawed and biased truth. In the introduction to "Trying to Save Piggy Sneed," John Irving warns readers that "to any writer with a good imagination all memoirs are false."

Minnesota Public Radio's Heather McElhatton discusses the issue of Truth versus Fiction in the Augusten Burroughs memoir *Dry*. Burroughs includes a disclaimer in which he says, "This memoir is based on my experiences over a ten-year period. Names have been changed, characters combined, and events compressed. Certain episodes are imaginative recreation, and those episodes are not intended to portray actual events."

McElhatton is okay with that, arguing that the work would have been ineffective as an 800-page journal. "Some say it is the storyteller's duty to stitch a pattern from reality in order to present a picture that can be truly seen."

I think consumers of memoir have to take some responsibility for fiction-as-memoir. Today's media-immersed readers expect to see story delivered cinematically, in-scene. They have little tolerance for long passages of narrative in which a writer summarizes and reports recollections from childhood. They want to be on stage with the players.

Real life is inefficient, disorganized, and sometimes baffling. It's also messy and cluttered with distractions that obscure the trajectory of story.

Sometimes real life doesn't work very well as fiction. It's hard enough to tell the truth without being hamstrung by the facts. I was in a critique group once with an older man whose novel was loosely based on his experiences as a government agent in the Cold War. "This isn't believable," we said, or nicer words to that effect. "Why would your character *do* that?"

"But it really happened!" he protested.

That's no defense. Strange as it seems, there are rules for fiction that do not apply to real life. As Tom Clancy says, "The difference between fiction and reality? Fiction has to make sense."

The memoir writer who wants to write a compelling story must impose some kind of framework on it. And that leads to accusations of fictionalization.

The fact is, in writing memoir, Job #1: to tell the truth, and Job #2: to deliver story effectively, are sometimes incompatible, depending on how you define truth.

In her book *Unreliable Truth: On Memoir and Memory*, Memoirist Maureen Murdock says, "The job of writing memoir is to find one's truth, not to determine the accuracy of what happened—that is history, a testimony, perhaps even an interesting tale."

If we insist on the truth, unaltered, uncondensed—we require memoirists to do an impossible job. Memoir is not a transcript, and we wouldn't read it if it were. Even the most fact-bound memoir is scarcely an unbiased report. Who has a greater stake in massaging history than the person telling her own story?

Even those memoirists who seem to delight in ripping the skeletons out of their closets and displaying them in all their gory glory still get to choose what skeletons they share and in what light. Ironically, as in the Frey case, they may be lying in order to make themselves look worse.

This damages the work. As a novelist or a memoirist, honesty is the only coin we have to spend. And fiction may be the best way to tell the truth.

Mimi Schwartz suggests that the memoirist gather what facts she can, then remain true to them while using the imagination to fill in the gaps. "If the main plot, characters, and setting are true, if the intent is to make honest sense of 'how it felt to me' and tell that true story well (with disclaimers as needed) it's memoir to me."

I'm okay with that. But I suspect that when authors include disclaimers about their memoirs, readers may zigzag through the story, pulling up short every page or so, saying to themselves, "Is *this* true? Okay, what about *this*?" If the intent of story is to immerse the reader, then it has failed.

Memoir is distinct from other types of non-fiction in that it serves the writer as well as the reader. The self-reflection required for memoir puts life events in perspective and helps the writer understand where she's been and where she is and possibly where she's going. Readers share in that self-discovery because some experiences are universal. As Patricia Hampl says in her book *I Can*

Reality-Based Memoir vs. Non-Fiction

Tell You Stories, "Stalking the relationship, seeking the congruence between stored image and hidden emotion—that's the real job of memoir." But writing frankly about real people and real events isn't always easy.

As a writer of memoir and personal essay, I have shied away from honesty at times when confronted with the pain of self-inflicted embarrassment, or the prospect of hurting family and friends. This interferes with the art and stunts personal growth.

At a writing retreat recently, a friend described her mother's reaction to an essay she wrote. In the essay, she described how a trip to Europe with her mother was a turning point in what had been a difficult relationship. Through writing the essay, she felt she had a new insight into her mother's motivations. When her mother read it, however, she focused on the troubled relationship part, expressing hurt and embarrassment. How will that affect my friend's ability to explore these issues through writing in the future?

There is also the very real possibility of lawsuits. *Running with Scissors* author Augusten Burroughs was sued by his adoptive family, even though he changed their names in his memoir. Although the novelist isn't immune to this ("I *know* that despicable character in your book is modeled after me!"), it is rare.

Why publish, then? Why not just write memoir for ourselves? After all, private journaling can be therapeutic and self-revealing.

In an article in *The Guardian*, memoirist Tim Lott describes "the deeply ambivalent reaction of the artist who both wants to share his private experience with an audience, and yet paradoxically—but genuinely—recoils from it at the same time." Lott suggests that the memoirist's motivation for organizing his thoughts and getting them down on paper is the desire to confess and memorialize—to honor the past. That requires sharing the work, and then struggling with the guilty conviction that he's betrayed and exploited those closest to him.

The temptation is to wait until everybody dies to tell the truth. And that works against the process of self-discovery.

For all of these reasons, I think the case can be made that fiction can be the better tool for telling the truth, delivering story, and helping readers and writers deal with the past.

Google "fiction vs memoir" and you'll find hundreds of hits, an immense controversy, and a wide diversity of opinion, with arguments ranging from shouting matches to hand-wringing debates.

Google "autobiographical fiction" and you'll find none of that.

I say, relax and write fiction. By all means, use your collected experiences to inform your work, what Tolkien calls "the leaf mold of the mind." But I believe that an author who stays offstage is more likely to tell the truth about herself and others. She will be less likely to succumb to the temptation to change, downplay, or exclude events involving real people who never agreed to be characters in her personal story.

In his novel *Hearing Secret Harmonies*, English novelist Anthony Powell says, "People think that because a novel's invented, it isn't true. Exactly the reverse is the case. Because a novel's invented, it's true. Biography and memoirs can never be wholly true, since they can't include every conceivable circumstance of what happened. The novel can do that. The novelist lays it down. His decision is binding."

Reality-Based Memoir vs. Non-Fiction

Fiction often reveals more about the author than memoir. As Mimi Schwartz says, "The seeming anonymity of fiction, even auto-biographical fiction, can be creatively freeing." We novelists feel safe under the cover of fiction. Like faces in firelight, we display thoughts and feelings we'd otherwise keep hidden. Sometimes we surprise ourselves. We reach onto our shelf of ideas, and pull down something familiar and at the same time unexpected.

I write young adult fantasy novels, which would seem to be the least likely vehicle for memoir. And yet, intentionally and unintentionally, they contain autobiographical elements.

My first three novels are set in Ohio, where I was born and where I live now. My sons' high school experiences inform many of the scenes in the books, and many of the major characters are based on composites of my sons and their friends.

But, to go deeper, I've noticed that in my fiction, the father is usually absent or plays a minor role. The mother is usually the strong parent figure. I don't do that consciously, but it happens over and over. I suspect it reflects my strong identification with my mother and my more troubled relationship with my father.

That's the unintentional part, and it tells the truth.

Fiction frees the writer to focus on story, on character, on the best way to deliver the truth. Unlike the memoirist, the novelist can strip away and condense what doesn't contribute—without having to defend herself.

In his blog, *Moby Lives*, Dennis Loy Johnson argues that in the face of the exaggerated memoir all around us, readers must look to fiction for authorial honesty.

As Pablo Picasso said, "Art is a lie that makes us realize the truth."

Point of view can be limiting in memoir. A talented memoirist has an eye for detail and a vivid emotional memory. But no matter how skilled she is, we can get into the head of only one person—the memoirist. In fiction-writing workshops, I caution students not to model a character too closely after a real person. We can never know another person as well as we need to know our characters. And that ability can add numerous weapons to the writer's arsenal.

Fiction, like memoir, can help authors and readers make sense of past events as well. In my most recent novel, *The Dragon Heir*, the viewpoint character, artist Madison Moss, is trying to leave the constraints of her Appalachian upbringing behind. As a fellow first-generation college graduate with Appalachian roots, Madison and her struggles have helped me sort out my ambivalence about my heritage.

I identify with Madison, as does a reader who wrote, "I've spent eighteen years trying to hide 'that' accent, to avoid the small-town sentiments and snap judgments people make when hearing or seeing something different. I knew exactly how Madison felt, about wanting to be more, but only seen as something else. Still, it felt good to be home."

I asked Hopkins about her decision to write fiction rather than memoir. She says she chose to write fiction to serve the needs of the story and its intended audience.

"To write my memoir, I would have had to write from my point of view," she says. "The book would find a better home in the adult marketplace, I think. And as for content, I wasn't there to see everything that happened, so the focus would have been much narrower."

So Hopkins embedded elements of memoir in fiction.

I think it was a good choice. I have written memoir and I have written fiction, and I argue that fiction can be a freer, more effective engine of truth than any memoir. Choosing fiction enabled Hopkins to speak to her target audience—teenagers.

Hopkins gets inside the head of her protagonist, the dual Kristina/Bree, and captures her voice. Because she is writing fiction, she can tell the story in scene—a more effective way to deliver it. We are in Kristina's head the first time she uses crank.

Fire!

Your nose ignites,

Flameless kereosene

(and, some say, Drano)

Laced with ephedrine

you want to cry

powdered demons bite

through cartilage and sinuses,

take dead aim at your

brain, jump inside

This format totally serves story.

Hopkins could tell her own story in memoir—the story of a parent whose child becomes addicted to crack. But she chose not to. "I really didn't want to write an 'Oh, poor me, my daughter is a drug addict' memoir. I wanted understanding."

Are there disadvantages, then, in writing autobiographical fiction?

Hopkins' *Crank* carries the standard fiction disclaimer: "This book is a work of fiction. Any references to historical events, real people, or real locales are used fictitiously." Still, Hopkins gets questions about how much in her novels is truth vs. fiction. "I tell them *Crank* is probably 60 percent truth and 40 percent fiction. With *Glass*, it's probably more like 70 percent truth, 30 percent fiction. It was also a harder book to write, because those stories affected our family so directly."

As with fictionalized memoir, questions as to what is true and what is made up will still surface, throwing the reader out of the story. But here the author has said, "Assume this is fiction. Those questions you have are your problem. I'm not trying to pull anything here."

This raises the question: If fiction tells the truth as well as or better than memoir, could someone without Hopkins' experiences with addiction have written *Crank* or *Glass*?

Hopkins thinks not. "I think all novelists bring pieces of real life into their work. But to write a book about drug addiction . . . requires some sort of firsthand (or at least secondhand) experience with drug addiction."

Finally, have Hopkins' books done the job of making sense of past events, for the author and the reader? The evidence says yes. Reader response has made both *Crank* and *Glass New York Times* bestsellers. Many addicts and former addicts write to Hopkins to say that the books tell the truth and have made a difference in their lives. These novels have reached teens in a way that an adult memoir would not.

Writing the novels has also helped Hopkins herself come to terms with her own guilt about her daughter's addiction: "I started *Crank* for me . . . as an exploration of why my daughter made the decisions she did and what part I might have played in those decisions. . . . I learned a lot about myself through the writing. The main truth I discovered, however, was that the choices my daughter made were HERS. She had the information, but made them anyway. My guilt load didn't vanish, but it lightened considerably."

Will Hopkins ever write a memoir? Maybe. But not until there is some real closure. And that hasn't happened.

"After six years clean, she relapsed a few months ago," Hopkins says.

She is still waiting for the end of the story.

Cinda Williams Chima began writing romance novels in middle school, which were frequently confiscated by her English teacher. She is the author of the *New York Times* bestselling Heir series of young adult fantasy novels. A graduate of the University of Akron and Case Western Reserve University, Cinda has been a freelance writer for the *Plain Dealer* and other publications. Cinda has a marginal knowledge of popular culture, but she has never forgotten what it was like to be a teen. Her new fantasy series, The Demon King, is set for release in fall 2009. Visit Cinda at www.cindachima.com.

PART II

Life was good
before she
met

        the monster.

After, we were
thrown into
the maelstrom,

        tattered,

tossed up against
a wall of pain
until it shattered

        our trust.

After she turned
away, slammed
the door, and

        left us

in her shadow,
still she sent
us tumbling,

        reeling

in the tail
of the tornado.

When BenBella asked if I'd be interested in a book of essays about *Crank* and *Glass*, I was, of course, honored. And when they offered the opportunity for my family to contribute, I was excited. Here was the chance to access the real "inner conflicts" of my husband, son/grandson, and daughters, including Kristina. I'm certain my readers will be appreciative, too.

The most interesting thing to come of their contributions, for me, was how they all chose to relate some of the same episodes, as witnessed through four different sets of eyes. I have already talked about how truth is colored by perception, and that is quite apparent here. Four themes surfaced. For my husband, anger, and how it never disappears entirely. For daughter Kelly, losing her best friend. For Kristina, how the overwhelming need to fit in drove her to do things that in many ways went against her nature. And for Orion, how the choices his mother made before he was born have shaped his life, even with her largely not in it.

I asked for this section to end with Orion's thoughts, rather than Kristina's, because I truly feel the story at the heart of *Crank* and *Glass* doesn't belong to her alone. It belongs to thousands of people who have chosen the same path. But more, it belongs to their families, especially the children whose parents have been taken away from them by one monster or another. And it is with the children that the real hope for a brighter tomorrow lies. The hope of Kristina's story lies with Orion, and his siblings, who have the power to use their understanding of the past to shape the future in a positive way.

Letting Go

John Hopkins ("Scott")

As I write this, a number of emotions surface. Disappointment. Hurt. Confusion. Anger. Mostly anger. I thought I had buried that anger somewhere in the seven years since our lives settled down again. But six years of turmoil can never be forgotten completely. I don't know if I can ever totally let go of my anger, which is the fall-out of love, dismissed.

All step-parents carry a certain burden. The first time I heard, "You're not my *real* dad" it stung. I entered "Kristina's" life when she was five and her brother was seven. Their own father wasn't around and hadn't really bothered to involve himself in their childhoods. I stepped into the role of stepfather with high hopes. By the time the events in *Crank* unfolded, I had come to care for Ellen's children in a tangible way only raising them could make possible: helping them with homework, comforting them when they were hurt, celebrating birthdays, suffering parent-teacher conferences, and cheering each role in school plays.

Together, we went camping. Fishing. Swimming. We took family vacations to the beach. Theme parks. Museums and monuments like Hearst Castle. We weren't exactly rolling in dough, but we made sure the kids had nice clothes and the latest toys. In return, we expected them to help out around the house and the garden, which was really another way we tried to stay connected. Ditto with the always plentiful pets: fish, cats, dogs. We had labs first, then German shepherds, all integral members of the family.

It was one of our dogs, in fact, who alerted us to a problem when Kristina was around fifteen. He woke me from a deep sleep by frantically scratching and whining at the bedroom door. "What the hell? Go away, Blitz."

Blitz would not take "no" for an answer and when a hundred-pound German shepherd insists on wanting out, you comply with his wishes. I stumbled down the hall, still half asleep. The dog stopped abruptly as I reached the top of the stairs. Blitz was not given to nighttime accidents, so what had begun as an isolated incident was becoming a bit strange. "Well, come on, dog."

Blitz held his ground outside my oldest stepdaughter's bedroom. Prancing a bit uncertainly, he looked like he was ready to pee right there.

"Blitz, let's go." Now fully awake and recognizing the impending hassle of dog urine at one in the morning, my commands were not befuddled but rather stern. The scratching and whining resumed, this time at Kristina's door. "What is it Blitz?" I studied the dog for a clue. No doubt about it. He wanted me to go in that room. "Kristina, you okay?" I called as I knocked on the door. "Kristina, wake up."

There was no response from the other side. Discarding prudence, I opened the door. Blitz charged into the room ahead of me and went straight to the window, which was open, screen peeled back. The bed was empty. Kristina was gone.

That dog was worth his weight in gold. Anxiously wimpering and gesturing with his paw, he and I shared the same question: What now? Had she been kidnapped? You'd think it would have made some sort of commotion; it was a second-story window. Any kidnapper going in and out would have had to be Spiderman. Yet, there was no reason to suspect she had run away.

Letting the dog out didn't require assistance, so my wife had remained in bed, though also awakened by the animal's gesticulations. She joined me now. "No way." Her immediate anger told me Ellen knew more than I did. "She wanted to go to a party tonight and I told her no. I bet she went anyway. Kelly will know where she went."

Down the hall at the next door, I held back as Ellen went into the bedroom. "She's gone too. I can't believe she dragged Kelly into this with her."

Three years Kelly's senior, Kristina seemed to be a late bloomer, but the bloom had begun and now, Kelly was striving to keep up with a best friend who was taking a different path. While the rebel in Kristina had reared her head on several occasions, there had been no indication that things had gone this far. "Do we call the police?"

Quickly dismissing the law enforcement option, a more devious plan came together. Turning out the lights, we took up residence on the living room recliners. In an apparently dark and sleeping house, we waited for the prodigal daughters to return. Stretched out at our feet, Blitz breathed a sigh of relief knowing Ma and Pa were "on it."

The dog heard her first. Blitz knew the game was afoot and alerted us without making a sound. Shortly after, we heard a couple of thuds from the area of Kristina's room. Then her door opened and she came padding lightly down the hallway, already in her pajamas. She headed for the stairs, not noticing us on the couch.

"You might as well turn on the light. We've been waiting for you. Where's your sister?"

The light clicked on and Kristina glared in our direction, looking as irritated with us as we were with her. "Downstairs. She snuck out and woke me up to let her in. Somehow the door got locked after she left."

Kristina had a habit of telling escalating lies through her childhood. Often times, the lie was a more serious offense than what she was lying about. As she descended to "monster depths" the lies were often times laughable but sometimes they were quite good and we were conned countless times. This one might have been believable if the dog hadn't given her up.

"Don't even go there. We've been in your room. You can pay for a new screen too."

"I'm not lying. She climbed out my window but couldn't get back up, so I'm going to let her in."

"Kristina, WE WERE IN YOUR ROOM. YOUR BED WAS EMPTY."

Ellen and I took turns sparring with her, our initial anger mixing with frustration as we tried to deal logically with Kristina, who was spewing lies faster than her mind could think.

It would be clean and neat storytelling to dramatically pronounce "and so it began." But it's hard to know when the con really began, or if it will ever really end. That first "bust" certainly opened our eyes, but given its similarity to events to come, and how well orchestrated it appeared, I think there had been prior trips out that window that ended successfully. There were certainly several more to come that we know of. Who knows how many times she went on a walkabout undetected?

Later, she adjusted her strategies, at least while she gave a damn about getting caught. It didn't take her long to figure out that the dog was sounding the alarm. Didn't matter if it was pouring rain or blowing snow, she'd put that poor dog out in the cold so he couldn't alert us. Kelly became an unwanted complication and was easily discarded.

As Kristina's friends changed and got rougher-looking, the distance between Kelly and Kristina grew. Their childish sisterly bickering became more vicious and at times even physical. Kristina finally stopped taking Kelly along at all. It's harder to keep the story straight if there are two people telling it. Kristina and Kelly's secrets became weapons of extortion against each other and their relationship became an elaborate dance. Kristina became more short-tempered and irrational. Consequently, the confrontations became increasingly heated and often ludicrous.

We began to suspect drugs were involved. The first tip-off was the smell of tobacco, always clinging to Kristina. She claimed it was from her friends smoking around her but her behavior signaled something worse, something deeper. Finally, we breached the trust we believed she had already broken, and went looking. A search uncovered cigarettes, and more. When confronted, she swore she'd never do drugs again: "I just wanted to see what it was like."

Not long after that, she went out the window on a Friday night and didn't come home. Enlisting Kelly's help, we asked all her friends if they'd seen her, and were met with a unanimous chorus of "No's". We were angry and frustrated. Nevertheless, we worried all weekend. Had she run off? Had she met the wrong guy and ended up dead in a ditch somewhere?

Finally, on Monday morning, her boyfriend (according to Kelly—Ellen and I had never met him) Chase called and told us Kristina had been arrested for post-curfew drug violations. She was in juvenile hall. Seemed she had given the authorities a fake name, thinking her friends could get her out. Who knew you actually needed a parent to sign you out of juvie?

Her arrest led to interventions and counseling sessions and community service hours picking up trash on the weekends. When her counselor asked her why she was behaving this way, Kristina told him she was sneaking out and doing drugs "to fit in." He replied, "And how does that make you special? The stoners will take anyone."

Amazingly, she managed to graduate. For many, graduation is a beginning. For Kristina, it was the beginning of a tailspin. Without the constraints of school, she soon took charge of everything she felt she should control—when to sleep (or not), when to eat (or not), when to go out, when to come in. The rest of the family was on pins and needles. We couldn't leave the house for fear of what would happen in our absence. We went out to dinner one night in December. While we were gone, Kristina threw a party and her friends all helped themselves to wrapped gifts from under our tree—a holiday grab bag.

Finally, we had enough. If nothing else, we were obligated to provide a safe and stable home for Kelly, who was still in school and showing her own signs of struggle and rebellion. We showed Kristina the door after an unusually intense argument, concluding that we could return to a normal life only if Kristina was living somewhere else.

Weeks would go by with no word from her. When there was word, she was always with a new man, each one progressively more felonious in deeds and appearance. Once, after an unexplained week-long absence, she was dropped off in our driveway by a man in a new BMW who did not speak English. Within minutes, she was picked up by a homeless-looking man in a beat-up pickup truck. Her teeth were rotting and her hair was falling out. For several months the story was that she was moving into a mansion (once it was finished being built) owned by the heir to the largest construction firm in the region. Somehow I doubted it.

It wasn't long before she was pregnant—but she had a plan. Apparently the father had proposed. She declined the proposal but they were together and it would be all right. Soon the child was born. It was a long and painful labor, which now seems just. Hunter was born much as he is today: a beautiful, healthy, and intelligent child.

One thing was immediately apparent, and became even more so as the weeks went by. Hunter was not black. Not even a little bit. The guy Kristina named as the father was black. Kristina's biggest con yet was in play but the guy stepped up to the plate and refused to flinch in the face of the curve balls and sliders Kristina threw at him. He even proposed again. Kristina, on the other hand, began leaving the baby with him while she dated other guys.

Finally, Kristina announced that he was not the father, that she did not know who the father was, and, "Uh, sorry 'bout that. Thanks for all the free babysitting you did while you thought you were a daddy. And by the way, meet the thug behind door number three, who loves me deeply and wants to adopt my baby."

Soon after she moved in with " Brad," his three children, and his mom, Kristina started having sex with her new beau's cousin, "Trey." Before long, the cousin also "loved her deeply and wanted to adopt her baby." Suddenly, to Kristina's surprise, the aunt, who had been the grandmother and now soon-to-be great aunt, didn't want them living under her roof anymore.

Kristina moved home for a while and went to work at the nearby 7-11. She would stay out almost every night, come in and change, go to work, come in from work, then go back out to party, until her body couldn't take it anymore and she would crash for a day or two. Ellen and Kelly played "Mommy" in Kristina's place as her interest in the baby faded more and more. While Hunter recognized her voice and strained to see her whenever he heard it, he was but an afterthought to her. It was heartbreaking.

One day I came home from work and Ellen was beside herself. Kristina was gone. Hunter was there. I asked what had happened. "I came in and the baby was crawling at the top of the stairs, screaming," she said. "Kristina was crashed out on the floor. I could barely wake her up. When I finally did, I was so angry I pushed her out the door and told her she was leaving, but the baby was staying."

Apparently, when Kristina asked where she was supposed to go, Ellen told her she didn't give a damn, that the baby's life was in danger while she was there, supposedly taking care of him. Kristina called a few days later and said she was out on the street. Ellen took a stand. She said Kristina could not come home, and suggested she contact one of her druggie friends for a place to stay.

So when Kristina showed up and announced she was taking the baby and getting on a bus to show him to Trey's family in Arizona, we put our foot down. We had been the only ones to show any interest at all in this baby's welfare (except for the man Kristina had originally claimed to be the father). Spending much time with her various thugs, Kristina had, without question, become a thug herself. The mutual tirade that followed was one of the worst. I told her to leave and not to come back without a cop. Given that she had become a "tweak of nature," there was little chance of that happening. We contacted a lawyer and took guardianship of Hunter.

Kristina and Trey set up housekeeping together. At one point, they almost burned the kitchen down trying to cook meth. Later,

Trey's best friend would move in, initiating yet another round of thug-hopping for Kristina.

But meanwhile, hoping to rekindle what had been a family, we invited Kristina to come with us and the baby to cut a Christmas tree in the nearby mountains. If she had a place for a tree, we would get a permit and cut one for her, too. Kristina double checked the time we would be gone and announced she had plans she could not get out of during that exact time frame. Or perhaps she was formulating plans.

It wasn't a week later that Ellen got a call from a local market. Seemed someone had tried to write a check on our account with a dubious I.D. When the store clerk questioned the I.D., the girl ran from the store leaving the check behind. Sure enough, someone had gotten to the box of checks in our office. But they didn't just grab all the checks, or even the ones on top. They took one booklet from deep in the box. That way the numbers would not jump sequence when we put new checks in our checkbook for several months. Acting on a hunch, Ellen went to investigate her jewelry box. She did not find anything missing from the box, mainly because she could not find the box—it was gone just like the checks. As our property was populated with several large German shepherds, access was limited. Any thief would have had to get by those dogs.

A few days after that, the mystery was solved when the newspaper published a surveillance photo of the girl that was passing forged checks around the city. It was one of the best pictures of Kristina I had seen in a while. It was now out of our hands. We had no choice about filing charges. The businesses where she "issued forged

150

instruments" all pressed charges and we had to report the burglary to keep from being held liable. I'm not even sure at this point if this was the beginning of or just another installment in her various jail visits, which grew into prison visits.

An interesting thing happened when Hunter turned three. He started calling Ellen "Mama," and me "Papa," instead of "Gamma" and "Ganpa." We had really been his parents all along. He understood that, and made the decision on his own. That was when we decided to forego the guardianship and adopt him. On the day the process was finalized, the family court judge thanked us for choosing adoption by giving us a crystal heart, signifying our family's unified hearts. We all cried that day, including the judge.

For Kristina, it was not a lesson learned. I'd like to say Hunter was the only child affected by her lifestyle, but she kept on having babies. I'd like to say things have changed. But the boyfriends continue to be thugs. The babies keep coming, with little apparent effort to provide a stable home and future for these children. Always living on the edge—evicted here, living in a weekly there—Kristina's current scene is, to quote a classic tune, "the same as it ever was." She claims otherwise, but I stopped accepting words without the actions to back them up long ago. Had to. We were all played for fools too many times.

While this all sounds very harsh, the anger has actually eased, though it is never far from the surface. I'd like to think that I have moved on and that the emotions so easily recalled are just that: a *recollection* of anger and tension. I don't often dwell on those years, but when I do, I can feel my heart rate quicken and a tense knot begins to tighten my stomach. My body physically reacts to the memory and it's scary to think that those feelings, which are hugely absent from my life today, were so commonplace ten years ago.

These events ravaged our family, but we have moved forward despite lingering doubts. We've left all (okay, most) doors open. Sometimes I look back and wonder what I might have done differently. But when I think about Kristina's childhood and all the happy times we spent there, I realize the best thing I can do now is to simply let go.

Best Friend, Stolen

Kelly Foutz ("Jake")

A best friend is someone you laugh with. Someone you cry with. Someone you share your most intimate secrets with, knowing they're safe. Losing a best friend is never easy. It's hard if they die, of course. But in many ways, it's even harder if they turn their back and walk away from you. And if your best friend happens to be the sister you love and admire with all your heart, the grief and resentment never fade completely.

I lost my best friend, my older sister, "Kristina," the summer she turned fifteen. She visited her dad for two months that summer. After that, nothing was ever quite the same. As she stepped off the plane, jealousy seeped from my every pore. She had changed a great deal. I noticed her tall, lean figure; her blond hair; her blue eyes—and what happened to the glasses she had when she left? She had traded them in for contacts, and now she wore makeup. She was really pretty. And I was really aware of it.

I myself was a little bit on the chubby side, with light brown hair and brown eyes. I saw myself as plain. I was twelve, and had little girl crushes on the boys in my grade. Soon, all of my childish days would end. I would force myself to fit in with the same crowd my sister did, and the days of playing with Barbies and My Little Ponies would be over. That night, I snuck down the hall to her room so I could hear about all of her private secrets. The ones she wouldn't share with anyone but me.

"Do you promise not to tell Mom?" she asked.

I promised, and we laid together on the floor, just like we had done so many times before, staring at the ceiling and whispering. Kristina showed me the new cross tattoo on the U-shaped piece of skin between her thumb and pointer finger. She also revealed that she had started her period, and met a boy. She thought then that he would be her forever love.

But it wasn't long before the local boys also began to take notice of my sister. We were hanging out in front of the 7-11, as most kids in our town did. That was really the only place for kids to hang out. A van with a bunch of teenage boys pulled up, and one of them, who my sister thought was "so cute," asked for her phone number. She gladly gave it. I was envious. This took place time after time, as she handed out her number to every boy who asked for it.

Kristina also confided that she had headed down her rocky path before going to her dad's. About halfway through her freshman year, she told me, she began hanging out on a curb across the parking lot from her high school. The place was first referred to as "the Avenue," and later as "Smoker's Corner." She started by smoking cigarettes and then some "pot," as she called it. She shared her experiences with me as we hung out or pulled weeds in mom's garden.

That summer was the first time we started sneaking out to go to parties. We waited until our parents went to sleep, and then Kristina would tiptoe into my room and we would go out my two-story window. We would put our feet sideways, creep across a piece of wood that was about an inch wide, and swing our bodies from the window to the deck. Though we both mastered the going-out part, only Kristina could make it back in. (To achieve the feat, you had to jump from the deck railing onto the small window ledge. She had the courage. I didn't.) This was the main reason we were caught so much. My sister would have to sneak through the house and unlock the door to let me in.

We partied regularly that summer, which was also when we met "Chase." My sister and I had hidden an extra telephone downstairs, and would ask our parents if we could sleep on the bottom floor of our house. We would plug in the extra phone and make phone calls in the middle of the night. I began talking to Chase, whom I had never met face to face, through an introduction by a mutual friend. He was seventeen and I was twelve. We talked for weeks. Finally, one night we agreed that I would sneak out. I didn't want to go by myself, so I begged Kristina to come along. After a lot of prompting, we snuck out together.

Chase was definitely less than desirable. He was overweight, with greasy red hair, and he wore all black; his favorite piece of clothing was a trench coat. He wore the same thing every time I saw him from that first meeting on. Chase took us to a party out in the middle of nowhere. The "leader" of the party decided that I was too young to be there with older teens and twenty-somethings, and he kicked us out. Chase apparently had a word with him that night, because I was allowed at all of the parties after that.

At the second party we went to, Chase introduced me to his sixteen-year-old cousin. I thought "Danny" was an angel. We sat and talked for a long while. Later, Chase asked me to come outside for a few minutes. He looked sad, and said that I was supposed to be "for him," not for Danny.

This party was very important because it was the first time that Kristina and I were introduced to meth. Some kids who had it in a bowl in front of them explained what it did and said it was "magic." We decided not to use it that night, but the kids at the party had it in great supply and were ready to share. Danny urged me to play Truth or Dare and said he would "keep me all to himself." During the game, Kristina walked in from a beer run with a much older man. That was when Danny saw her. By the end of the night, he would claim her virginity. I was very angry, because my twelve-year-old mind thought Kristina had taken him away from me.

The romance between Kristina and Danny didn't last very long. Soon, she was going out with Chase. She dated him on and off through the school year, and into the next summer. Chase went as far as to drive more than two hours to where we were vacationing so Kristina could sneak out and be with him.

On Kristina's sixteenth birthday, we lied to our parents and told them that we were spending the night at a friend's house. We actually went to a party Chase threw for her out in the middle of the woods. Everything was going along just fine, and then at the end of the night, I went looking for Kristina. I found her in the center of a circle, bleeding. The others had cut her arm. I was really scared.

"It's okay," she told me. "They need to drink my blood, so I can be part of the brotherhood."

I kept telling her not to let them, but she insisted, so I left the area and fell asleep on the hood of a car. Later, I found out what the brotherhood was. According to Chase and the other "brothers," everyone in the group had to share or drink each other's blood. This made them part of a pact. When they all grew up, one of them might be a doctor, one might be a police offer, etc., and they would help each other out, according to what they did for a living. Kristina refused to drink anyone's blood, so she cut her finger and rubbed her blood on a poster with swatches of the other member's blood.

This was when Kristina, my best friend up to now, really began to pull away from me. She started using meth with Chase, and did not want to tell me anything about what was going on anymore. When I went to her room to talk, she was always tired, and yelled at me to go away. She shut me out for the next couple of years.

One night in mid-December when I was fourteen, my family was all going to the movies. Kristina said she felt sick, and we left her home in bed. Everything seemed fine until Christmas. A lot of the gifts were missing, and we didn't know where they were. John kept asking what happened. Finally, Kristina cracked and admitted that she had invited some of her friends, including Chase, over the night we had gone to the movies. They had stolen our Christmas gifts. After some threats from John, Chase brought back the presents, which were already very well-used. Chase lost all of my respect at that point.

Just after this incident, Kristina came to my room crying. It was very late, and she was clutching her stomach, telling me how bad she hurt. I could not even conceive what was wrong as she crawled into bed beside me. Worried, I rubbed her belly and told her to wake up Mom. She was really afraid to go to our parents, but after awhile, she did because the pain was so great. Mom rushed her to the emergency room. Turned out she was having a miscarriage. I was shocked. Our parents didn't take it lightly. She was grounded for the next several months. Not that *she* seemed to know it. Grounded or not, she kept right on sneaking out.

When I started my freshman year of high school, Kristina was a senior. This was when "the stoners" really began trying to pull me in. I didn't fit into any other group, so I began to hang out on Smoker's Corner. I never really tried any hard drugs, but I smoked cigarettes and marijuana. Sometimes I would steal all kinds of candy, backpacks full, just to have something to give to my new friends. Kristina and her pals urged me to steal more so they would have stuff to eat during their munchie cravings. They offered me meth more than once, but I always refused it. Kristina and I argued all of the time, and I started to wonder what had happened to my best friend. I was covering for her more and more, and began to feel that was all I was good for.

That one year that we were both in high school together passed. Sometimes after school, we would go over to Danny's house, which he shared with several roommates. We would all smoke pot together for long periods of time.

Just after graduation, Kristina confided that she was pregnant. She was only eighteen. She urged me not to tell our mom or John and said that she was going to have an abortion before they ever found out. I strongly disagreed with her decision, and voiced my opinion. I told her that her baby already had a soul, and it was wrong to kill it. She told me that it was not my body, and it was her decision. Before she could do anything, I went and told our mom she was pregnant. I'm not sure if it was because Mom found out or what, but in the end, Kristina decided to keep the baby.

About this time, I started dating Keno, the boy that I would go out with for the next two years. We got married when I turned eighteen, and we're still together ten years later. He was all I thought about, day and night. I guess that's how most sixteen-year-olds are. Kristina and I spent even less time together then, and the rift between us grew wider.

Soon after Kristina had her baby, Orion ("Hunter" in *Crank* and *Glass*), she moved in with a man named "Brad" to take on a position as nanny. Brad was in his late thirties, still lived with his mother, and had three children. Best of all, he could get meth easily, plus he paid her well for babysitting. They were romantically involved for a time. But, never satisfied with one guy for very long, Kristina began a romance with Brad's nephew, Trey, who was staying in the same home. She later told me that he left her love letters under the soap dish in the bathroom and in other hiding places. As soon as Brad and his mother found out about Kristina and Trey's relationship, they told her to leave.

One night, Kristina and Trey drove up to our parents' house. I was staying alone for the weekend, because our parents were wine tasting a few hours away. Kristina asked where they were, and I told her they weren't home. I remember that her breath smelled like a rotting body, and her pupils were huge. "You need to take the baby," she said, pushing him into my arms and hurrying off, leaving no time for argument. I stayed home from school the next day and cared for him until my parents returned.

Not long after that, Kristina moved back home with us. Orion was four months old. Having the baby around was fun at first, but then it started to feel like a chore—changing him, feeding him, playing with him, etc. Kristina never seemed to take an interest in him. She would lie around and sleep for long periods of time, and she would cuss at the baby when he cried. She started using my parents as a babysitting service.

One day I was in my room with a friend. Kristina came in and offered us meth. We both said no. She kept pestering me, calling me a prude, until I finally relented. I refused to snort it, so she put some into a cup with soda and I drank it. A short while later, I felt jittery. I had an urge to talk, walk, or do something active. I asked my mom to drop me off at Keno's, and while I was there, I cleaned their entire house, which was quite unlike me. Cleaning was definitely not my favorite thing. That night on the phone, I confided to Keno that I had tried meth. He told me that he was very ashamed of me, and that if I ever did drugs again it would be the end of our relationship. His response was a real wake-up call. I realized he was more important than drugs, and I never tried any again.

For some ridiculous reason, Kristina thought she was in control of the situation. She never really understood that pretty much everyone in the family knew that she was using again. One night she said she was going out. Our parents said no, but she insisted. This sparked a fight, where she threatened to leave with Orion. John took a stand. He said she was free to leave, but not with the baby. In the end, whatever she was leaving for was more important than Orion. From that time on, my parents raised (and ultimately adopted) him. That turned out to be for the best, on many levels.

For a while, Kristina and Trey were homeless. I'll never forget the day I was hanging out at the sandwich shop where Keno worked and Kristina and Trey came in. They had not eaten for several days and begged Keno for some food. He loaded them up with sandwiches, chips, cookies, and sodas (all of which he paid for, out of his own pocket). Kristina called our parents several times, and they agreed to help her, but not Trey, because he kept providing her with drugs. Kristina always refused help for herself. The two kept on using meth. On a whim, they decided to go to the courthouse and get married. We didn't find out until after the fact and then only because Mom happened to notice their marriage announcement in the newspaper.

Eventually, they both went to jail for selling drugs. After they got out, they stayed in a weekly motel, and worked their way up to an apartment. Every time we saw Kristina, she was thinner, her teeth were more yellow, her complexion was worse, and she looked sicker overall. She would disappear for weeks at a time without telling us where she was. And then she was pregnant again, this time with a baby girl.

About two weeks after she had the baby, she asked me to watch her so that she and Trey could go out for New Year's Eve. When it was time to go to sleep, I started to rock the baby. Each time her eyes closed and I put her down, she would wake up screaming frantically. I remember thinking how odd the baby's behavior was. Most newborns sleep a lot, but this baby was afraid to be left alone. I was up late into the next morning, until my sister came to get her.

I really never got to know that baby, and neither did my parents. Kristina had her until she was almost two, and after that I never saw her again. She went to live with Trey's family in Arizona when Kristina and Trey went to prison again, this time for fraud. Kristina was locked up for two years. When she got out, she was harder. Meaner. A stranger, really.

So that's how I lost my best friend. When my mom started to write Crank, I wasn't sure how I felt about her sharing our story with the world. But over time, I've come to understand why she thought it was so important. If this can be my family's story, it can be anyone's. Only by comprehending the nature of addiction can we avoid and/or overcome it.

My overall thoughts on Crank and Glass? Wow! My mom sure did know a lot! She knew the key players much better then Kristina or I would have thought. The two books really get at the main point—meth ruins lives in a major way. It gets way down deep into the cracks of your spirit and poisons you to the core. It rots you from the inside out. It darkens the best parts of your life until they are gone. You can no longer see what is important. The drug reaches out and grabs everyone it can.

Kristina may have started using fifteen years ago, but the effects can still be seen today, even though she is clean. With the first snort, her bright future was gone. She was hooked. She stole from family, friends, and total strangers. She ruined people's credit, and hurt and manipulated innocent people.

It was not my best friend doing those things, though. It was not the beautiful, blond-haired, blue-eyed girl that I had once been so close to. It was the monster inside her at work. It stole a mother from her children, a daughter from her parents. It stole a sister and friend from the people who loved her, and robbed society of a smart, important person. We can never have her back the way she once was. I hope, through reading *Crank* and *Glass*, that others will turn their backs on the monster. No amount of popularity or fun is worth losing your soul.

Kristina Speaks Up

"Kristina"

I'm not exactly sure where to begin, but to describe where my heart was at the beginning and how it got lost along the way. Any way you look at things, I'd like it to be known that I've always wanted to do the right thing. Even when it came right down to destruction and carnage in my wake, I looked upon myself in a kind of helpless and detached way: a flailing passenger on a tumultuous runaway train destined to destroy everything in my path, knowing my own demise will be eminent upon encountering the slightest obstacle yet unable still to do anything but watch on autopilot and hang on for dear life.

I don't blame anyone for my actions, or try to blame a bad childhood for my faults—in all actuality, I had a very privileged upbringing. I didn't really see it as such, being your typical teen-ager, but my problems weren't anything to put into a storybook. I believed I was "blooming" when I began acting out, and I really did create a kind of alter-ego to carry the guts-and-glory part of things through. Without that part of me I may have actually become vale-dictorian and gone on to college. It's a tiny bit scary that this same me could quite possibly have been a judge or lawyer and responsible for defending or condemning the very same kinds of people that I ultimately became, isn't it?

My only reason for showing little to no resistance to the dark side was yearning. Deep and mourning within my soul lived a desire so desperate to be assuaged that it consumed my dreams: I wanted to be accepted and embraced by the other kids more than anything in the world. I looked at the pretty girls and wanted to look like even the plainest of them so that I would be accepted and admired and fit in. I longed for the cruel little tyrants to like me, but I had glasses and straight-As and had not yet come into any real maturity, even by the end of the eighth grade, when all "those" girls had boyfriends and went to parties. I suppose a child of any age with a traumatized heart becomes easily malleable when her deepest desire becomes a possibil-ity. When it comes down to a search of the soul, I suppose I would even go so far as to say that I still feel the desire for attention and approval from anyone in my vicinity. I've fought to reach a point where most of me is so far beyond that cosmetic crap it's unbelievable, yet that one little seed remains at the back of my skull, nagging my brain like a tiny parasite. And sometimes it surfaces no matter how hard I fight it, or how far beyond shallowness I believe I have advanced.

Kristina Speaks Up

Everyone grows up eventually, and as I became more and more willing to throw all caution to the wind it never occurred to me to stop and take a look at myself. My transformation came almost overnight, and suddenly one day the boys began to notice me. Well, one boy at first, but after that they came almost too easily. The "bad boys" called to me like the sirens of myth and lore called to sailors, and each step I took toward them led me further and further astray. I still saw myself as the ugly duckling, and each flirtation built my confidence to new levels. I had finally found my own power and that, in itself, was the first and most addictive drug in my arsenal of self-destructive weapons.

Still, for some reason I couldn't fully see that I had magically become an actual beauty. It was like some unseen force kept a shroud over the person I had become, and every flaw I possessed became magnified in my mind and heart, until I reached a point where I obsessed over each tiny thing and constantly felt incomplete—always striving for greatness in the eyes of others and constantly failing to ask myself what could make me happy with myself. In the middle of my freshman year, I adopted an iron-clad façade of a trend-setter. I clung to the disguise for so long that, after years of putting up a front, I actually finally figured out how to believe in the fictional person I created. In doing so I found liberation. I realized that people didn't want a weak-minded little girl that simpered at their feet and rushed to please. They wanted "Bree," as my mother so aptly named her, the self-confident leader of the pack who wasn't afraid to speak her mind and didn't give a damn what they thought of her or anything she did. And that is exactly who I showed them. I pretended to be a self-confident, mellow "stoner" who started trends because my style was the only one that mattered.

Of course, Bree was an entirely made-up person. I decided to let surface an exact opposite of who I felt I was, and amazing things began to happen. The girls stopped trying to beat me up, and then went out of their way to make friends with me. Ironically, they fell over themselves to please me because I successfully made them think I couldn't care less if they liked me or not. I couldn't believe the difference in their attitudes and actions. That made it even more important to build my walls of smoke and mirrors so they would not find out that the only reason I "liked" certain music, clothes, hobbies, and people was because they did. I lived alone inside myself because I was afraid to draw the attention to myself that might send my carefully mortared walls tumbling down as a result of lack of structural integrity.[1]

So this was where my soul fretted when I reached the first really bad decision to be made—the first of the evils that led me down a shadowed path and dragged many friends and loved-ones through the depths of my abysmal undertow.

It seemed like a harmless thing to smoke a cigarette, a deliciously bad little habit to hide from my mom and stepfather, one that would immediately curry favor among the popular and make me feel as if I had taken a huge step toward liberation. Truth be told,

---

[1] I think most people act in whatever regrettable ways they do because of fear—lack of trust in the humanity of the human race. We're just all too ignorant to open our eyes to our true motivations, and too self-centered to care about anything more than our own skins first and foremost.

I actually went through a kind of indescribable misery to accomplish this feat of stupidity. I realized, after trying to fake smoking for a week or so, that I looked like an obvious poser. After all, a true smoker can see when somebody doesn't inhale. The first time I inhaled nicotine into my lungs I didn't even cough, and this, of course, boosted my confidence, and I happily smoked an entire cigarette immediately before classes began at school. I felt fine and I fit into the group like I had always belonged there. My spirits soared! The bell rang and we filed in to first period like we did any other day, but my heart was pulsing with a kind of jubilant song. For the moment, nothing was even remotely amiss in a place where anxiety normally prevailed.

Ten or fifteen minutes into my English class, my euphoria ended abruptly. My face broke out in a cold sweat and my limbs began to shake. I got up from my chair and ran like Satan himself was at my heels. I made the bathroom, but was a long way from the toilet. I spewed things I swear I ate for dinner three or four nights prior, and bawled like a newborn as I splashed the floor and wall with filth I can't even begin to describe. When my gut was finally emptied I felt much better, but I knew right away what had made me sick and dreaded the days to come. I wondered if smoking would always cause this reaction and feared the answer, yet continued on my path with perseverance. I found out in the most awful way that some people's bodies take about two weeks to adapt to the strength of the nicotine bombarding them before they develop any kind of addiction or immunity, but still I pressed on in the same daily fashion until I woke up one day and realized I needed a smoke. The whole journey to that point had kept me wondering how in the ever-loving hell people could get hooked in the first place if the price was so high.

This was kind of the way I progressed through each bumbling experiment, first with booze, which I hated, and then with marijuana, which I abhorred. I continued to misuse both with single-minded purpose, however, because I refused to be deterred.

Both pot and alcohol made me feel detached from the world. "In a tunnel" is the sensation my sister and I used to describe the experience. Being intoxicated in these ways filled me full of dread because I hated feeling helpless and out of control. I had to know I was completely in command of my mind and able to retain my sanity and my disguise or I constantly feared for my adeptness in the crowd. I was forced to carefully control my own usage while convincing others I was using far more pot and alcohol than I actually was, which is not an easy feat. I also detested feeling dizzy and nauseous and, once again, could not see what all the hype was about or why on God's planet people got off on being helpless and flailing on the carpet. They actually bragged about passing out in their own vomit, but I could not stomach the thought of showing signs of weakness. I was already lost in a world I couldn't fathom, and I didn't even realize yet that life, as I had it structured, was very soon about to crumble.

Shortly after I turned fifteen I decided the next logical step toward destruction would be to get losing my virginity out of the way. Not because I had any desire for the sexual aspect of things, but because I was sick of being the "odd man out" when sex came into any discussion. It didn't take long to do just that, but I didn't feel any different when it was all said and done. I didn't achieve the desired epiphany. The fantasy that girls have about their entire life having meaning once they become a woman was all a load of crap, and I became even further disillusioned. There was little to no enjoyment for me in sex. Somehow, I had led myself into a trap that now left me obliged to get the tedious chore out of the way before I could build any relationships or be taken seriously. I never even knew what kind of enjoyment a female could find in the whole business until I was much, much older. As a result, I sank deeper into bleakness.

By the time I was nearing seventeen years old, I had let too many things fall apart on the surface. I was careless with my schoolwork, and aroused the suspicions and anger of my parents with almost frightening frequency. I behaved in appalling ways at parties and just in general. Even thinking about some of these things now is downright embarrassing. Suffice it to say that my mother was very on-target with a good number of the assumptions in her story. One of the things I found most amazing was how she intuited who the "good guys" and "bad guys" were. For instance, without really knowing (and definitely without liking) "Chase," she seemed to know he really did love me, and had my best interests at heart.

But there was so much more she never imagined. Like the fact I not only trafficked meth, but also manufactured it heavily for awhile. Or like the time one of the guys[2] I moved in with pulled out a gun and shot someone right in the head. I was standing not two feet away, and the sight messed me up for years. It would take thousands

---

[2] This guy was also the chemist who showed me how to cook meth.

of paragraphs to relate them all, and I'm not sure I have the courage to confess every secret. I do know this: at first the horror stories I heard about crank were sufficient to keep me afraid and I swore I would never breach the line between harmless drugs like weed and dangerously addictive drugs like speed. I stayed away because I was terrified of overdose and brain damage and everything else that has been attributed to any controlled substance that comes in a white or powdered form.

I truly wish that whatever genius launched the DARE program would cease whining about the dangers of pot and put some real effort into scaring the daylights out of would-be methamphetamine enthusiasts before all hell breaks loose in their lives. Because it wasn't at all hard to break my resolve when some friendly peer pressure was applied to just the right places.

In fact, considering how hard I fought to avoid breaching the divide up until that point, it was really easy. And once I crossed the line there was no prayer of turning back. What's truly and sickeningly funny is that I often bragged that I didn't have an "addictive personality," using this lie as a cover for not getting completely hammered during past forays into less frightening vices. I hadn't the slightest clue how wrong I was.

For some reason, in the midst of the blurred haze that encompasses a sizable portion of my past, I remember everything about the first time I tried crank, down to the smallest detail. I sat in my friend's old Pontiac, squished in with four of my closest comrades in the parking lot of a slimy old bowling alley, and I watched as they made four smallish lines on a cracked CD case. My best friend,

"Robyn," goaded me to try a little. I resisted, mostly because I was afraid of the burn, but I hated the thought of being the only one not included in the party. Finally, she persuaded me to snort a tiny blast made from the remnants of the other lines. That way if I didn't like it, the effects wouldn't be nearly so powerful.

I caved in like a virgin on prom night. I felt almost no pain from the initial impact, and almost instantly my heartbeat increased and my spirit leapt in a way that made me feel truly in control of my own destiny. I was hooked, and I wanted—no, needed—to know how far I could go and what heights I could achieve. Suddenly, crank became the world's most harmless little drug in my mind, so as to more easily justify each time I dabbled in the wondrous euphoria that made me feel alive and helped me believe my uncertainties had been vanquished.

As with any addiction, at first it was a once-in-a-while pleasure, but it became an all-consuming passion before I even had time to wonder how I got lost in the grip of the monster. I found, for a time, a substance that sated my great hunger to feel totally in control, and common sense lost its foothold. I have countless regrets and hundreds of memories that would make the strongest man's skin crawl to hear them recounted. I may find the courage to completely purge my demons when there is more blank paper and hours of time in which to search my past. The story has not been completely told yet, and I would not want to ruin any surprises that "Kristina" has yet to relate, but just know that there is no such thing as easy fulfillment of your greatest desire. There's a reason that God does not always give us everything we ask for, and that is most people don't really know what they want. Fewer still have a clue what they actually need.

I put myself through the darkest drawn-out hell anyone could possibly imagine, and I dragged people with me who should never have had to experience pain inflicted by my hand. I'm filled with deep remorse. Meth poisoned more than my body. It poisoned my life. I am ashamed of what I allowed it to do to me and to my integrity. I can only hope that I will be able to keep others from making the same mistake. If I can prevent even one person from taking the same path I have then it all will have been worth it. No matter what the struggle these days, I comfort myself knowing that I have been through worse things, and anything else that could possibly get thrown at me from this point on will be a learning experience and nothing more. My soul is at rest and it's become a bit easier to find a smile in the tiny beautiful things that life has to offer.

There's no real way for me to travel the universe attempting to save people or anything, but I suppose that's not my intention anyway. I just want a few people to open their eyes and see the possibilities that surround us, but are overlooked more times than they are noticed—to understand more fully the repercussions that can be incurred so easily with a seemingly unimportant little dalliance. And maybe to appreciate just a little the things we so often take for granted.

I've spent years tearing at my bindings again and again only to design yet another oubliette to puzzle through until I find the chink in the bricks and can begin anew to tear them down. I travel in circles like a diabolical carousel in a horror novel. But I have finally found freedom in the ability to battle my demons and win. My world has become a lovely place because I appreciate each and every moment of life not spent in the hands of the monster. Oh, now don't get me wrong—I still dream about him from time to time. I still miss his kiss and the escape from pain that he offers. I still think about getting high just one more time so the world will make sense for a heartbeat or two, but I have found the strength to fight him off, for which I am eternally grateful.

I urge you to never forget that addiction is not easily controlled, and very rarely completely beaten. If you're already in recovery, never be so sure of yourself that you take the wrong risk and get pulled back into oblivion. The hunger will hit you when your back is turned. Learn to see that life is the most precious gift and if you piss it away you'll wake up one day and realize it's over before you ever got a chance to really live. Do your best to find joy in the sunshine or a rainbow or in the simple smile of another. If you succeed you will feel a weight lift from your heart.

There's a universe full of endless promise. It carries many pitfalls and there is a price that must be paid, but if you look only for the good in things, you'll find that the bad won't tear you down nearly so thoroughly. Discover your wonder before it becomes too fleeting to capture long enough to know it was even there.

Choices

Orion Hopkins ("Hunter")

Hi. I'm Orion. I'm eleven years old, and I just started sixth grade. You might know me as Hunter, the baby from *Crank* and *Glass*. That story isn't one I wrote for myself, and my mom didn't write it for me. It's one I lived, but not one I chose.

My mom, by the way, is really my grandmother, but as long as I can remember she's been "Mom" to me. She says I used to call her Gamma, but that was so far back that I don't remember it. She and my dad (Scott in the books) have raised me since I was a baby. They adopted me when I was four, so they really are my mom and dad. Adopted parents may not be your biological parents, but they are your real parents because they take care of you and are there for you.

I do know "Kristina." Over the span of my lifetime, I can remember her visiting maybe ten times, mostly at Christmas. My aunt Kelly has been a much bigger influence in my life. In the books, she is "Jake." Mom says she changed some characters to allow them privacy. I don't think that worked out so well, because so many people know the story now.

The story is my mother, Kristina, left me with my grandparents and aunt so she could go out and use drugs. The drug she liked best was crystal meth. I don't know that much about meth, except you can get addicted to it after using it one or two times. It must be expensive because one time Kristina broke into our house and stole stuff so she could get money for it.

I think I was two the year that happened, so I don't really remember it. But I've heard the story many times. Mom, Dad, Kelly, and I went up into the mountains to cut our Christmas tree. Mom says they invited Kristina to come along, but she said no, she had things to do. We still go cut our tree in the mountains, so I know it takes most of the day. While we were gone that day, Kristina and her friends broke in and took video equipment, Mom's jewelry, and some checks. Later, Kristina went to jail for writing those checks and signing Mom's name.

I do kind of remember the next Christmas. I was waiting and waiting for Santa to come. One night I woke up. People were yelling and our dogs were barking. I stood up in my bed and looked into the hall. A big guy was walking and pushing another little guy. I got all excited, thinking the big guy was bringing presents. But when I asked, "Is that Santa?" my mom came into my room. She said, "No, honey. Santa doesn't come until tomorrow night."

When I was older, I found out the little guy was a friend of Kristina's who had snuck into the house when everyone was asleep. He was looking for Kristina, who didn't live there anymore. Aunt Kelly slept in Kristina's bedroom then, and he got into Kelly's bed. She was so scared, she got panic attacks for awhile after that. I also remembered the big guy was wearing a green uniform, not a red suit. He was a deputy sheriff.

I'm telling you these stories to show you how the choices Kristina made have shaped my life. When I started kindergarten, I was five. Sitting still and concentrating was not my best thing. (It still isn't, but I've learned how to do it better.) The teacher thought I had ADD, because she knew Kristina was using meth when she was pregnant with me. She wanted to give me drugs for ADD. My mom and dad didn't want me to take drugs, but the teacher found some herbal stuff and they said, okay we can try that.

All those "vitamins" did was make me nervous and angry. I remember feeling so angry. It was like everything bad in my life boiled up all at once. Luckily, my mom noticed and told me to quit taking the herbal vitamins. The only reason any of that happened is because of the teacher's prejudice about my past. She was trying to help, I guess. But she also wanted to make things easier on herself.

The thing I feel saddest about is having a brother and sisters who I don't get to see very often. I haven't seen Jade (the baby Kristina is pregnant with at the end of *Glass*) since she was two and I was four. I'd like to know her, but we don't even know where she is right now, except she's with "Trey's" sister. I've seen Heaven, who was born after Jade, exactly once. She lives with her father's parents. Clyde has been to our house three times, at Christmas. Kristina had him after she got out of prison and he just turned four. Clyde does have some behavior problems. He's hard to control and has been tested for autism. I don't know if that's because of drugs or what. It doesn't matter. He's getting help now.

I don't want you to feel sorry for me. My life is good. My mom and dad love me a lot. We travel to cool places. We ride quads and go skiing, camping, and river rafting. I get decent grades and am a Boy Scout, which is fun. I know I'm better off where I am than with Kristina. I've seen how she lives, barely getting by and never really finding the right person to love. I think that's sad, and it's mostly because of the choices she made when she was a teenager.

I'll be a teenager soon. I'll have choices to make, too. My mom and dad have talked to me about addiction. I know I'm "predisposed" to it. That means because Kristina was addicted, and her dad also had addictions, I could easily get addicted, too. So I'll always have to be careful about how I decide to have fun. My parents will be looking for the signs, too. And they'll probably look harder than they might have if this hadn't already happened to them before.

Sometimes I think they're already a little stricter than they need to be. Like they're trying to avoid problems before they happen. Maybe that isn't fair, but I do understand why. I've already decided to stay far away from drugs, but I can't promise to be perfect. Everyone makes mistakes. I'll just have to try and keep mine small.

From the *New York Times* bestselling author

Ellen Hopkins

Crank
"The poems are masterpieces of word, shape,
and pacing . . . stunning." —*SLJ*

Burned
"Troubling but beautifully written." —*Booklist*

Impulse
"A fast, jagged, hypnotic read." —*Kirkus Reviews*

Glass
"Powerful, heart-wrenching,
and all too real." —*Teensreadtoo.com*

Identical
*"Sharp and stunning . . . brilliant."
—*Kirkus Reviews*, starred review

Published by Simon & Schuster